Pity The Dead

Detective Solomon Gray, Volume 5

Keith Nixon

Published by Gladius Press, 2019.

One

No need to bother, sir. Just another dead junkie.

That was the message Detective Inspector Solomon Gray had received less than half an hour ago, only a gulp of coffee into his morning shift.

He was at his desk as usual, buried under paperwork (literally it felt like, recently) and sick of being stuck in the office. Gray's DI role was to oversee the portfolio of investigations underway in CID and ordinarily he'd have left the case to his team.

But not this time.

This time he made his way to the chalk cliffs on the edge of Ramsgate. Because the man's identification had meant something to Gray. A memory from his past.

Archie Nolan.

Gray absorbed the scene. The corpse sat upright on a bench within one of the five ornate wooden promenade shelters built by the Victorians. The shelter was a rectangular box of carved wood and plate glass with a wide open entrance set into the cliff. A place to take a leisurely rest and admire the sea view, not to die in.

The promenade itself was a concrete sea defence wide enough to drive a car along, maybe a quarter of a mile long and some six feet high. It ran east from Ramsgate's main sands towards Broadstairs before abruptly stopping. Every few hundred yards steps were cut into the concrete, leading onto the beach of sand, rocks and pools. Beyond lapped the brown waters of the English Channel which were low and quiet, the tide on the turn.

Now, like much of Thanet, the shelters were past their best. Broken glass, graffitied wood, flaking paint. At night it was pitch black here, no artificial lighting within hundreds of yards. A little illumination spilled over the cliff edge from street lamps which bordered the formal lawns and flower beds of the Winterstoke Gardens above, but the shadows were deep and dark. Here the underclass gathered to be away from the watchful eyes of others. To shoot up or have sex. Maybe even both.

Just a junkie.

Gray remembered Nolan from way back. He'd been at nursery then school with Gray's daughter, Hope. Nolan had visited Gray's house on many occasions, for birthday parties and play dates. Once they reached their early teens Nolan looked on Hope differently but she was oblivious to his unsophisticated intent, too absorbed by music and too little time for boys.

Then one day Nolan just stopped coming round. Gray never knew why and Hope didn't clarify. Gray wondered whether Hope, who was living a whole different life now – married with a baby daughter herself in Edinburgh – would recall him at all.

Probably not.

"When are Crime Scene Investigators due to arrive?" asked Gray.

"The skemmies should have been here already," said Detective Constable Jerry Worthington, who'd transferred from his home town of Newcastle in the north east of England over a year ago. "I'm sick of doing nowt." He kicked at a stone and sent it skittering off the promenade onto the beach.

Worthington was a large man with dark wavy hair and stubble on his chin who retained his broad Geordie accent. The tattoo of his home football team was just visible beneath his short sleeved shirt, the weather still warm in September. Worthington liked to work out and the shirt stretched over prominent muscles.

"Skemmies, constable?" asked Gray. Worthington's choice of words sometimes threw him.

Worthington rolled his eyes. "They're pigeons, bad ones. You know, pecking away at the floor, looking for crap. Like CSI do, sir." He shoved hands in trouser pockets. "And I told you there was no need to waste your time."

"Don't worry, Jerry," said Gray. "You'll still be SIO."

Gray had no intent of taking over as Senior Investigating Officer, he had enough to deal with already. Worthington snorted but the lines on his forehead lessened. He winked at DC Melanie Pfeffer, a recent recruit and also an incomer, transferred from the Home Counties. Her surname had been Preston when she'd arrived but she'd changed it shortly after.

Where Worthington was tall and dark, Pfeffer was petite and blonde, the style short and easy to manage. Under five feet tall and a good twelve inches shorter than Gray. She was maybe half his age – mid twenties if he remembered correctly – and athletic in build. Pfeffer wore the usual ghost of a smile on her face. She had a tendency to stare, her blue eyes rarely blinking. Gray had noticed her several times seemingly looking at him across the Detective's Office. The thing was, he quite liked it.

"What's the hold up?" asked Gray.

"Maybe they don't think he's worth their effort?" shrugged Worthington.

Another dead junkie.

In the last couple of months Gray could recall at least five similar deaths across the region. Five anonymous men and women who'd been found lifeless, died by themselves in grubby locations. All were ruled as accidental; overdoses. Their 'entertainment' had killed them. Quickly resolved cases, brief coroner investigations, anonymous funerals. Not unusual for Thanet, an officially deprived area with more than its fair share of problems.

"How was he identified?" asked Gray. He doubted there would be a wallet on the body, or any form of formal documentation.

"Somebody rang in that there was an OD," said Worthington.

"They named him as Archie Nolan?"

"No, by his street handle, Lippy. The local beat cop made the connection."

Lippy – perhaps it was irony and he never talked. Or maybe too much. Gray remembered Nolan as being sociable.

"Have you examined the body?"

"Only to check for a pulse. Cold as a bottle of beer straight from the fridge, sir."

Gray noticed Pfeffer briefly pulling a face behind Worthington. The expression had been one of disgust. Gray had to agree with Pfeffer's judgement. And he knew Worthington was exaggerating. Once the heart stopped beating the body began to lose heat; about 1.5C per hour until reaching ambient temperature. Known as the death chill.

Another outcome from the heart no longer pumping was rigor mortis, when the limbs stiffened. And then settling of the blood as gravity took hold. All of these could be used to estimate the time of death, but that was a job for the pathologist.

Gray moved closer to the corpse, watching where he stepped, being careful not to contaminate the scene. He paused a couple of feet away. Nolan was seated on the bench, slumped against the inner wall. His eyes wide open, staring at nothing. Rubbish had blown into the corners of the shelter; crisp packets, sweet wrappers and a burger box from a popular fast food outlet.

It was difficult for Gray to recognise the schoolkid he'd once known. Nolan's haggard features were twisted into a grimace of pain. His skin as pale as the chalk cliff above, as the blood drained down. He was young, in his very early 20s, but looked a decade older. Years of living on the streets and repeated substance abuse.

A rancid odour arose off the cadaver even from here. Gray breathed through his mouth. This wasn't the stench of biological decay. This was a different kind of degradation; of someone who wore the same clothes, who washed rarely, who cared more for the rush of narcotics than their own health. Body odour, halitosis and faeces; the latter resulting from the bowels relaxing after death. Nolan would, quite literally, have shit himself. Another spoonful of ignominy.

One of Nolan's sleeves was pushed back, baring the forearm.

A needle, syringe attached and the plunger all the way in, just below the elbow.

A strip of rough dark material hung off his arm, like it had been wound around the muscle, kept tight by him gripping the material between his teeth.

A tourniquet to force the vein to stand proud, released once the drugs kicked in and exploded into his body, the vein no longer needed.

"Sir."

Worthington's outstretched arm pointed in the direction of Ramsgate. An ambulance rolled along the concrete promenade. No blue lights, no rush because there was no need. Behind the emergency vehicle without a crisis followed a car which Gray recognised as belonging to the local pathologist, Dr Ben Clough.

Moments later, both vehicles drew up a few feet from Gray's vehicle. Clough got out first, paused beside the ambulance, waited for the driver to lower his window before saying something brief then carrying on to Gray's team.

"Morning, Sol." Clough, a wiry man with sharp features, gave Gray's hand a quick shake. His skin was chill to the touch, like he was one of the corpses he inspected. Gray had long ago got used to the feeling, but it was clear Worthington had not. When Clough released his grip on the DC's hand, Worthington wiped his palm on his trousers. The pathologist appeared not to notice, his attention focused on the new recruit. "I don't believe we've met before," said Clough.

"DC Pfeffer."

"From your surname I'd guess you're German. Am I right?"

"Well, I'm English, sir," said Pfeffer, "but my heritage is Jewish."

A spark of irritation twitched Worthington's face. There and gone fast, but noticeable enough to Gray. He wondered what the source was.

If Gray were honest with himself he knew little about Pfeffer. Since her arrival, when he'd publically welcomed her to the team, standing at the front of the office, getting everyone's attention and giving her a brief introduction, they'd barely spoken. Gray had been too busy.

"My apologies and pleased to meet you." Clough shook her hand also. "And it's great to have you on board. We could do with somebody sensible around here." The pathologist released his grip, turned to Gray, the obvious target for his jibe, and said, "Let's take a look at what we have."

"A dead junkie," said Worthington. "Obviously an overdose."

Clough raised a palm. "Leave the drawing of conclusions to me, please."

Worthington gave a low bow. "How about I buy us some scran to say sorry?"

"Thinking with your stomach again?" said Gray.

"I'm a simple lad," said Worthington.

"I'll take a coffee if you're offering," said Clough.

Worthington turned to Pfeffer. "Coffee and bacon sandwiches all round then, Mel. There's a kiosk back in town on Victoria Parade. You'll have to walk though." Worthington patted his pockets. "And I left my wallet on my desk." He threw her a fake smile, all teeth, no emotion.

"I'd be happy to," said Pfeffer.

"Good lass. That's what I like to hear."

Pfeffer was new to the area and Gray suspected she didn't know where Worthington was sending her. "Come on," said Gray. "I'll show you." He made a mental note to have a word with Worthington in private about his treatment of Pfeffer which bordered on public humilation.

"I'm okay, sir," said Pfeffer.

"I insist. Jerry can keep an eye on proceedings."

"I'm happy to do the real work. Might get me that vacant sergeant's slot. And besides," said Worthington with a smirk, "Lippy's not going anywhere soon."

PFEFFER STAYED SILENT during their walk towards the kiosk. Gray had to initiate the conversation. A few years ago she'd have been deemed below the minimum height restrictions to join up. But these days recruitment was tough. Being a cop anywhere was no cushy number, much less so on the island.

After a couple of minutes Gray glanced sideways at Pfeffer. "How are you finding Thanet since your move down, Mel?" he asked as they neared the steps which would take them up the cliff and to the road above.

"I prefer Melanie, if that's all right, sir."

"Of course, no problem."

"It's just DC Worthington who insists on contracting my name despite how many times I've asked him not to. One day he might just get a kick in the balls. And as for Thanet, it's different, sir."

"Herefordshire was your previous patch, right?"

"Nearly, sir. Hertfordshire."

Not nearly at all. One was on the Welsh border, largely rural and the least populated county in England, the other a London overspill of wealth and privilege.

Gray stopped asking questions while they climbed a set of stairs against the cliff. Thanet was pretty much flat, any incline shallow and short. Gray had spent some time in the Derbyshire Peak District a few months back. They had proper hills there. Pfeffer trotted up the steps, two at a time where Gray was slower.

The cafe stood a few yards from the chest-high metal railings running along the cliff edge. It was a small rectangular wooden construct painted white with flaps raised to expose the counter and inner workings of the kitchen. Two tables and four white plastic garden chairs sat just to the right. By the time Gray reached the clifftop, out of breath, Pfeffer was leaning against the kiosk wall.

She turned her head as he neared. "Will Dr Clough want anything to eat?"

"Just the coffee. No food while he's working."

"Noted," said Pfeffer. She returned her attention to a skinny balding middle-aged man with his back to her while he worked the coffee machine. She said, "Just that then, please."

Another, much younger man was flipping bacon on a hot plate. He was tall, thin also. The cook put the sandwiches into a bag, placed it and three Styrofoam cups onto the counter.

Gray reached for his wallet but Pfeffer was already there. "I've got this, sir." She handed over some cash, took the change. "Want a seat?" she asked. "There's no rush, as DC Worthington said."

"His bacon will go cold," said Gray.

"Hardly our fault, is it?" Pfeffer gave the hint of a smile. Gray couldn't help but return with a grin of his own.

Gray sat, watched Pfeffer extract one of the rolls and peel the lid off two styrofoam cups, the liquid inside steaming. She handed one to Gray said, "Black coffee, no sugar and brown sauce in your sandwich, as you like it, sir."

Gray felt a tinge of embarrassment. Pfeffer aware of his habits yet he couldn't reciprocate. "Bacon is off the menu then?"

"Yes." Pfeffer paused as she was about to bite into her roll. "What's the matter, you're looking at me like I have two heads."

"Sorry, I didn't mean to."

"Jews aren't vegetarians, if that's what you're thinking. It's just the meat has to be kosher or I won't touch it. It's not a case of making a choice between chicken and pork."

"Oh, sorry."

"Lots of people get that wrong," shrugged Pfeffer. "Including DC Worthington."

Now Gray realised why Worthington had taken visible pleasure in sending Pfeffer here – to impact on her religious beliefs.

Gray ate half his roll, wondering what to say next. He wasn't the most adept of communicators and for some reason he didn't want to come out with anything which might sound stupid. Eventually he said, "You changed your name recently. Did you get divorced?"

Pfeffer laughed. "I'm not the marrying kind, sir. I don't even have a boyfriend."

"Sorry, I didn't mean to pry."

"It's all right, sir. What about you? Are you in a relationship?"

Gray was, but hardly anybody knew. His partner was a cop too. "No time." Only a partial untruth. Gray drank some coffee. "So, the reason for the alteration?"

"I reverted my surname to what it used to be. Many Jews Anglicised their identities around the time of the Second World War. Pfeffer's my original family name."

"Can I ask why?"

"I'm no zealot, before you say anything."

Gray raised his hands. "I used to attend church so I understand the demands faith can put on a person."

"Quite." Pfeffer paused, perhaps trying to line up her thoughts. Gray studied her face, noticed a small mole beneath her lower lip. "It's simply that since I moved here I've struggled to fit in. The only friends I've been able to make are other Jews. But there aren't many of my people in Thanet. There's hardly even a *minyan*." Pfeffer must have seen Gray's look of confusion as she said, "To hold a service there has to be ten or more males present. That's a *minyan*."

"Okay."

"I've been talking to Rabbi Rothschild quite a lot. Eventually, I realised it's the history we should preserve."

"Fair enough."

"You don't attend church yourself any more, sir?"

"I lost my faith. I'm glad yours strengthened." Gray put the lid back on his coffee. "We'd better be getting back."

"Hang on, sir." Pfeffer leant over, touched Gray on the thigh. He tried not to flinch. She glanced inside the second cup she'd removed the lid from. Hardly any steam was rising. "We're good. Worthington's is about right now."

BY THE TIME GRAY AND Pfeffer returned to the scene Nolan's corpse was sealed up in a body bag and being wheeled towards the ambulance. Clough was putting his case onto the back seat of his car. Worthington leant against the railing, arms folded to accentuate his muscles, the beach behind him.

"I'll get you my report as soon as I can," said Clough to Gray as he straightened and slammed his door shut, "but based on my initial observations, and as DC Worthington surmised, an overdose is highly likely to be the cause of death."

"Told you," said Worthington.

Gray ignored him, said to the pathologist, "Thanks Ben."

Clough gave a jaunty wave and began to reverse along the promenade, allowing the ambulance to move off too.

"You took your time," said Worthington, holding his hand out for the refreshments.

"They were an age preparing everything," said Gray.

Worthington bit into his sandwich, pulled a face. He peeled apart the bread and glanced inside. "Hadaway man, there's brown sauce in here!"

"I asked for ketchup," said Pfeffer, holding her hands up in surrender. "I'm sure they'll replace it if you go back."

"Give me that coffee so I can get rid of the taste." Pfeffer passed over the Styrofoam cup. Worthington removed the lid and took a large gulp. "It's lukewarm and there's no sugar." Worthington wagged the roll at Pfeffer, his cheeks colouring. "You did this on purpose."

"She didn't," said Gray before Pfeffer could speak. "It was busy."

Worthington glanced between Gray and Pfeffer then shook his head. "What a bloody waste."

Gray caught Pfeffer's tiny wink as Worthington turned away and tossed the roll and coffee into a nearby bin.

Two

The title 'Odell House' could conjure up an image of a grandiose and stately building. Instead, the Margate police station was designed more for function than aesthetics, resulting in a three-storey rectangle of pale brick walls and white PVC windows overlooking the sea at the top of Fort Hill. The station was actually named after a police constable who'd lost his life in the line of duty nearly twenty years ago, though Gray would bet few locals remembered the event now.

Gray's intent when he entered his office was to review any information held on file about Nolan. Being an addict, he was more than likely to have history with the authorities. Probably relatively minor but time-consuming crimes like theft and burglary. It was fairly typical for users to feed their habit that way.

However, as Gray was halfway through entering his system password there was a knock on his open door. He shifted his attention away from the computer screen to Police Constable Damian Boughton, the station's severe weather vane.

Boughton was dressed as usual in police-issue trousers, boots and short-sleeved shirt, revealing faded tattoos from his time in the Royal Navy. If he ever covered his arms while on the beat his colleagues knew to hunker down because a storm was coming, though now was September and the late summer climate would continue for another few weeks yet. On Thanet the winters were typically mild, spring started early and the summer was warm enough to turn the lawns yellow and the ground hard before August.

"Come in, Damian," said Gray.

Boughton glanced around as he stepped over the threshold. "How's the new abode?"

"I hate it," scowled Gray, eliciting a chuckle from Boughton.

"That lot think it's great." Boughton hiked a thumb over his shoulder towards the CID team seated in the open plan.

Since Gray's promotion was formalised, his boss, Detective Chief Inspector Yvonne Hamson, insisted he have an office. Initially, he had resisted, retaining his desk outside with everybody else. Then, when he'd taken a few days' holiday, he returned to find all his stuff shoved into the cubbyhole he now occupied.

Complaints to Hamson fell on deaf ears (it was her who'd ordered the move to happen, after all). Gray had found little support from his colleagues who were glad to have him shunted out of their space and had actively participated in the process of shifting his stuff.

The only personal possession in Gray's office was a framed photo of his daughter. The picture, which sat on his desk, showed a grinning Hope holding his first grandchild, who she'd named Katherine, after her mother. In the background was the peak of Arthur's Seat, the hill which overlooked Edinburgh. Gray had taken time off for her wedding.

He pointed to a chair in front of the desk. "Take a seat."

"It's just a quick one, Sol. I heard a body was found earlier, down on Ramsgate promenade?"

"That's right. Archie Nolan, aka Lippy. Probable overdose. Did you know him?"

"Only of him." Boughton shifted from foot to foot.

"What's bothering you, Damian?"

"There's something going on."

"What?"

"I'm not sure." Boughton scrunched his face up. "I can't put my finger on it."

"I need more than that."

"It's best if I show you. Can you come out onto my patch?" Boughton's beat was central Margate, just a short walk from the station.

"I don't know. I've a lot on."

"I wouldn't be here take up your time if I didn't think it was important, Sol."

Which was true. Boughton wasn't given to histrionics. He was solid, reliable. "When?"

"Now?"

"Sure."

"My shift's over so let me get changed first," said Boughton. "We'd hardly blend in with me in uniform."

BOUGHTON, WEARING TRAINERS, shorts and a faded Duritti Column t-shirt led Gray out of the station. He turned down the hill towards the Turner Contemporary, a free-to-enter art gallery conceived more than a decade ago in a drive to regenerate the area. So far the results had been mixed; the Old Town, a vibrant assortment of quirky shops, cafes and restaurants, had benefitted, but the cash hadn't spread much further.

There were visitors from London, but most didn't stay long. Those who fell in love with the idea of living by the sea relocated within a circle of other like-minded DFLs – Down From London – with similar personal circumstances, creating a two-tier society. There was even talk of a DFL opening a fee-paying private school just along from Odell House, an idea which had caused outrage locally. Overall, unemployment on Thanet remained high and inward investment by large corporations was non-existent. In fact, companies kept pulling out of the area, exacerbating the situation.

Boughton, walking quickly, headed along King Street, Gray following, and cut through the Old Town, past a pub called The English Flag on one corner of the square. The Flag steadfastly resisted the pull of gentrification, reminding locals and tourists alike of what Margate had been before the gallery arrived: rough, ready and run down.

As the pair exited the Old Town and hit a busy main road Boughton waited for Gray to catch up then said, "I hope you're coming along to The Britannia for a beer next week, Sol."

It was Boughton's fiftieth birthdayand the pub was next door to the station. Gray would have preferred going to The Flag, even though the regulars weren't keen on cops. "Of course. Wouldn't miss it for anything."

They paused at a bank of traffic lights beside a huddle of 1970s-designed buildings which housed the District Council, law courts and library. "Good, I've only invited a select few."

The fug of diesel fumes caught in the back of Gray's throat. They crossed over and entered an area of mown grass and sculpted trees called Hawley Square.

Paths cut across the public space in a baseball diamond shape. Large Regency houses, four storeys high, enveloped the square on three sides. Once this had been a wealthy locale for the middle and upper classes. Now it was offices and multi-occupation flats.

Boughton pointed towards one of the wooden park benches laid out periodically around the edge of the square. Boughton sat, draped an arm along the back of the bench and crossed one leg over the other. He appeared relaxed and enjoying the morning sun. Gray joined him and glanced around, wondering what they were here for.

"Just soak everything up for a few minutes," said Boughton. "Tell me what you see."

Puzzled, Gray did as Boughton suggested. Eventually he said, "There's a couple of dog walkers, one mutt being particularly yappy, a mother pushing a baby in a pram, an office worker smoking, banished from his company to stand on the pavement." Gray shrugged. "Everything seems normal to me."

"But it's not," said Boughton. "I misled you slightly. I should have asked you to look at what you *don't* see."

"I'm still not sure what you're on about, Damian."

"You've been stuck in that bloody office far too long."

"Maybe you're right." Gray had known the DI role would keep him off the streets, doing what he enjoyed. He'd seen others go through it before, after all. But he hadn't realised quite how much he'd miss being directly involved in an investigation.

Boughton planted both feet on the floor, placed an arm on one leg and leant forward. Like Rodin's 'Thinker' sculpture, just with more clothes on. "Use your cop eyes, man. Where are the dealers? Where are the scallies looking for a fix?"

Now Gray saw what Boughton meant. Hawley Square, despite its outward appearances, was a gathering point for the shambling addicts and the pushers who satisfied their needs. Usually groups of drug users were seated at the very bench Gray and Boughton occupied, either going up or coming down off a high. But there were none. Boughton nodded as he saw Gray understood.

"What's changed?" asked Gray.

"I've worked here most of my career. I've more experience of this place than anyone else in the station. All your new CID recruits, they're from the outside." Boughton waved a dismissive hand, making it sound like an immigration argument. "They don't have a feel for Thanet, how it ticks now, how it's changed, who the key players are. Stuff like that."

"I get it."

But Boughton wasn't finished. "And they're not here to stay either, so really, do they care about digging in the mud? I've already told some of your lot about this, but they wouldn't listen."

"Who?"

"That Northern prick, Worthington. He said I didn't have a clue what I was on about. He's definitely not invited to my bash and I wouldn't mind if he was one who did clear off soon."

"Jerry's not too bad."

"He's an idiot." Boughton shook his head. "Stop defending him."

"Get to the point, Damian. What's going on?"

Boughton huffed. "People are afraid, Sol. They don't talk like they used to. I don't hear as much. But what I do know is there's a new supplier in town, a gang who use fear and intimidation to keep their business locked down."

"Drug-related crime has dropped, though." After several years of increases in burglary and assaults Thanet had seen a reduction of late.

Boughton snorted. "Hamson will assume it's down to Pivot, right?"

Pivot was a special team assembled to tackle County Lines gangs supplying drugs from the city into urban areas. The operation had been run by an outside team, headed up by Detective Chief Inspector Adam Yarrow. Emily Wyatt, Gray's clandestine girlfriend, was part of Pivot too. The team was currently operating up in Colchester, Essex.

"Me too," said Gray.

"Then you're *both* wrong."

"Where's the proof?"

"That's exactly what Worthington said. 'Show me the evidence.'" Boughton rolled his eyes. "But I've something better." He patted his stomach. "My gut instinct. It's what I feel. You need to listen. The rules of the game have changed, we just haven't recognised it yet. This lot, they work on a whole new level to what we're used to. And I think they might be connected to the dead druggie from this morning."

"Which new lot?"

"I'm not entirely sure. I only know they're Eastern European. You need to listen to me, Sol."

Gray took in the stiff expression on Boughton's face. "All right, I'll do what you suggest."

"Thank you." Boughton released a lungful of air, like he'd been holding on for too long.

"But I need more than just your instinct."

Boughton paused, thought briefly. "There's someone you could speak to."

"Who?"

Boughton shook his head. "I need to persuade him first. Give me a day, maybe two and I'll be in touch. Okay?"

"All right."

Boughton held out a hand which Gray shook. "Thanks," he repeated. "It means a lot that someone cares."

Three

This time when Gray sat down behind his computer nobody interrupted. He accessed the Police National Computer database. In the search options he entered 'drug related deaths' and selected the last six months as a review period before hitting the enter key. The software chewed away briefly before displaying a series of file links on Gray's screen. He clicked through one after the other.

After a few minutes Gray sat back, not quite able to believe what he'd read. Across Thanet as a whole there hadn't been five deaths as he'd thought, but eighteen this year. Make that nineteen including Nolan.

He filtered the information to determine that eight were female, the rest male. All resided locally, though three were of no fixed address. They were of a variety of backgrounds, ages, ethnicity and age. Initially, he could detect no obvious pattern connecting them, other than all were ruled accidental deaths as the result of an overdose. He sought the toxicological analysis, but couldn't find any references.

Gray had worked in Thanet since graduating from police college, most of it in CID. Based on his experience, nineteen bodies in just a few months felt much too high. To confirm his suspicions he accessed records going back three years. The comparaison showed six to eight overdoses over an annual period was typical, if that was the right word. So, at the highest rate in previous years that was, on average, 0.66 of a death per month. Now, it averaged at 2.11 – more than triple.

Gray went to his door and scanned the Detectives' Office. Tucked into the corner was a small kitchen area. Worthington was there, rattling a spoon in a mug. Gray headed over. The work surface was chipped formica with a kettle, a jar of coffee, pot of sugar next to a microwave, which Worthington regularly used, filling the area with the piquant odour of reheated curry. There was a sink too and a fridge underneath.

Worthington happened to turn around as Gray was approaching. "Want one, boss?" asked Worthington, raising his mug.

"I'm all right, thanks."

"Your loss. What can I do you for?" Worthington grinned, clearly amused by himself.

"I was talking to PC Boughton earlier."

"Why were you wasting your time with that loser?"

"He's an experienced officer, Jerry. He told me about an increase in drug overdoses. I just checked the data. Deaths are way up on normal."

"Aye." Worthington shrugged. "So?"

"This is the first I've heard about it. And from a guy on the beat, not one of my own officers."

"I didn't think they were worth bothering you with, given how busy you've been."

"They?"

"Druggies, low lives. They brought it on themselves, anyway."

"Did you know any of these people, constable?"

"People?" Worthington blew onto his coffee, took a tentative sip. "And no, sir, I wouldn't want to." He shrugged. "But what can we do about it?"

"Investigate, Jerry. Find out why there's been a spike." Behind them a phone rang.

"I guarantee every one of them was a radgie with a record as long as your arm, sir. A handful more off the street makes our lives easier, right?"

"Sir." Gray ignored the voice from behind. He clenched his fists. Worthington was still smirking. "Sir." A tap on the shoulder now. Gray twisted. It was Pfeffer, interrupting Gray before he could ram Worthington's words down his throat. "There's a call for you."

"Take a message please, Melanie. I'll call them back."

"Okay."

Gray took a deep breath. Pfeffer interposing had forced him to check himself. "Damian Boughton reckons there's been a change out on the street since Pivot."

Worthington rolled his eyes. "What does that old plod know?"

"I'm a similar age."

"There you go, sir." Another grin. "Boughton is just flapping his mouth. Has he got any proper evidence?"

"His experience."

"I thought you wanted us to operate on physical information and data, sir." Gray didn't answer, Worthington was right. He continued, "Of course there's been a change. Pivot took out whole supply chains. Crime is down. We're doing a really good job, sir and given our manpower issues there's hardly the time to look at the meaningful stuff, never mind some arsehole who's done themselves in."

Worthington looked beyond Gray, a scowl developing on his face. It was Pfeffer once more.

"Sir, message from Sergeant Morgan on the front desk," she said.

"I'll leave you two alone," said Worthington, taking his opportunity to move on.

"We're not done with this," said Gray to Worthington.

"Sure." Worthington kept walking, a wave over his shoulder.

"What is it Melanie?" asked Gray, his tone a little sharper than he'd intended.

"Somebody called Mrs Myerscough was trying to reach you. They said it was extremely urgent. Apparently you know her." Pfeffer passed over a small yellow square. The glue on the post-it note stuck to her finger briefly.

"Never heard of her."

"Sorry, sir," said Pfeffer. "Can't help with that one."

Gray headed back to his desk and dialled. The call was picked up after a handful of rings.

"Hello?" A woman's voice, high-pitched, out of breath, like she'd been running. Gray didn't recognise the voice.

"Mrs Myerscough?"

"She's just here, who may I say is speaking?"

"DI Solomon Gray, Thanet CID."

"One moment, I'll hand you over."

Another female voice came on the phone. "Solomon, so glad I've reached you at last. I need your help. There's no one else I can ask."

"I'm sorry," said Gray. "Who is this?"

"It's Sylvia." Gray only knew one Sylvia, but it couldn't be. "You've forgotten me already, Solomon? I was Jeff's PA." God, it *was* her. "Are you there still, Solomon? I need your help. My husband has disappeared."

Four

Gray pulled up on The Parade, a road which ran parallel to the beach front in Minnis Bay, at the southern edge of Birchington. The Parade was effectively a sea defence with a road built on top of it. Should the wall be breached the properties for hundreds of yards behind, built on lower ground, would flood. This was an exposed area, often battered by storms. On the far side of the wall a footpath stretched from Ramsgate at one end, all the way round the fingertip coastline of Thanet, through Minnis Bay and then to Deal to the west.

Gray looked in his rearview mirror saw a static caravan park and the towers of a ruined church, abandoned years ago when the ground nearby began to crumble into the waves. The church had been built adjacent to an ancient Roman fort. Long ago this was an important and strategic location.

Birchington itself had been a vibrant village until the beating heart was removed; the post office closed down, then the high street followed. These days Birchington was just a silent village with more than its fair share of pensioners.

Engine idling, Gray checked the address Sylvia had given him. She lived on Canute Road, a few hundred yards from the seafront and opposite the curiously named The Dip; a grass-covered bowl with sloping sides that kids would have fun rolling down, ten or more feet deep. It was like a sunken playing field.

Gray drove the remaining distance, turned the car onto the drive and parked behind a shiny BMW M3 with private licence plates. He sat for a few moments, staring at a double-fronted detached house. A climbing plant, maybe wisteria, draped across the width, between the upstairs and downstairs windows. Green leaves, no flowers. The front garden was neat; trimmed grass and borders filled with mature bushes Gray didn't know the name of. He was no gardener, a major reason he lived in an apartment block.

Sylvia had been Detective Chief Inspector Jeff Carslake's personal administrator and Carslake Gray's friend. Both were past tense. Because Gray made a discovery about Carslake and his history that rolled over their relationship like a tsunami, leaving utter destruction in its wake. Carslake was dead now – Hamson had been promoted to DCI while Gray moved to the vacant DI position Hamson left behind.

With Carslake's passing, Sylvia resigned and Gray hadn't seen or heard of her since. He hadn't missed Sylvia either because while she worked at Odell House they'd shared a mutual antipathy. So the surprise of hearing her voice and the request for his help still sat with him. Sylvia had only ever attempted to cause Gray trouble and he assumed nothing good would come of their meeting. He owed her nothing. He'd come here out of curiosity which he was now regretting.

As Gray moved his hand to the gearstick to put the car in reverse a face appeared at the huge front window, a splash of white, then it was gone. Gray paused. The front door opened. In the entrance stood Sylvia.

Ordinarily she was a well-groomed woman, somewhere in her 40s or early 50s. Gray couldn't tell and he'd never asked.

Externally at least, she appeared just as smart now. Wearing a white pencil skirt, a floral silk shirt and flat shoes, hair done up in a beehive style which must have taken time. Sylvia's eyes were usually hard and piercing. Not now. There was makeup down her face – tear tracks.

Gray sighed, turned off the engine. He felt compelled to follow up with her now. When he got out of the car, he caught the sound of breaking waves. The warm, salty wind whipped at him.

"I thought you weren't coming in," said Sylvia as he approached. Her eyes were bloodshot.

"Finishing a call," lied Gray. He stepped into a hallway of pale colours.

"Would you mind talking your shoes off?"

Using his heel, Gray pushed off his shoes without needing to bend down or undoe the laces. His feet sank into deep, plush carpet. He kicked the shoes to one side. Then Sylvia stepped out of the way, allowing him to enter. He thought he could smell of alcohol on her breath.

"Straight on the left," she said.

The front room was a warm, welcoming space, the walls painted a soft yellow. The carpet here was equally thick. A wood-burning stove set into one wall beneath a mantlepiece was unlit. The window Gray had seen Sylvia at gave a magnificent view towards the sea.

"Sit down, Solomon." Sylvia pointed to a matching set of leather chairs and a sofa. "I'll make you a drink, coffee if I remember right?"

"I'm fine thanks, Sylvia. I'd just like to know what this is all about?" Gray was keen to be done.

Sylvia lowered herself into the seat opposite. Beside it was a small wooden table and a crystal tumbler half full of a clear liquid. She lifted the glass, put it back down again without drinking. "My husband, Jasper, has gone missing."

"I didn't know you were married."

"We've been together for a couple of years, but only tied the knot a few months ago. Just after Jeff died. Sorry I didn't invite you to the ceremony." She gave Gray a humourless smile. "I changed my name to Mysercough."

"There's a lot of that going on."

"Sorry?"

"When did you last see Jasper?"

"He prefers Jas," she said, as if her husband was nearby and she was talking for him. "Yesterday morning. He was up and out before I got up, which isn't unusual, but he didn't come home last night. I tried his mobile. It went straight to voicemail every time. I think it's switched off."

"Where does he work?"

"Jas is a freight forwarding manager at a haulage company called Langham's on the outskirts of Dover."

Gray knew Dover, but not the company. "What time would he normally leave?"

"He's a morning person. Usually he's off by 6.30am to avoid the traffic. He works long days, it might be 8.00 in the evening before he gets home. All overtime, though and he's well paid. We always make the most of our weekends."

"When did you notice he wasn't home?"

"This morning after I got up. I sent him a text last night telling him I had a headache and I was off to bed. That was about 9pm. We have a spare bedroom and Jas goes in there if it's a late one, rather than disturb me. So it didn't bother me at all until I went in and found the bed unslept in."

"Maybe he'd made the bed himself?"

"Oh no." Sylvia shook her head emphatically, enough to make her beehive wobble. "That's my job. And I got up early, so I could make him breakfast. If I don't cook he doesn't eat. I took him a cup of tea and stuck my head around his door. But the room was empty. There's an en-suite and the shower was dry and all his clothes are still there. He didn't come home, Solomon, I'm telling you. I'm really worried."

"He's been gone less than thirty-six hours."

Sylvia lifted the glass and now she drank; two fingers worth of the booze. "This isn't easy for me, Solomon." Gray said nothing, let Sylvia continue in her own time. Eventually she said, "We've had some difficulties in our relationship. Arguments, things like that. Sometimes we bicker." Bickering seemed a trivial word to Gray compared to what she was suggesting about their current situation.

"When I first met Jas he seemed very confident and sure of himself, but as I got to know him I realised it was all an act. He was actually a mess inside, constantly on the edge. Occasionally he'd tip over, disappear on some bender. I'd worry myself to death, waiting for him to come home. Then, with a lot of love and attention from me, he got better. I was his rock. But recently, he's got bad again and him leaving, it's like the past. I've no idea what's happened."

"Why did you call me specifically, Sylvia?"

Sylvia drained the booze, placed the glass on the table slowly, carefully. "I don't like you, I never have. But you're a good detective and you won't stop until you've got an answer. That's what I need."

"Nice and frank, Sylvia."

"Why be anything else?" Sylvia reached behind a cushion on her seat, extracted a piece of paper and held it out towards Gray. He stood and took the photo, a head and shoulders shot of a portly, silver-haired man delivering an insincere grin to the lens. Myerscough hardly looked the picture of health. A heavily creased forehead, blood veins on his cheeks and a bulbous nose. He had the appearance of a drinker.

"I want to know where Jas is," said Sylvia. "Please find him for me, Solomon."

GRAY WAS DRIVING PASSING Westbrook on Canterbury Road when his phone rang.

"Can you talk, Sol?" said Emily Wyatt, Gray's partner, her voice loud and strong over the speakers.

"I'm in the car, so no problem."

"All alone for once, that makes a change."

"You forget, I've got an office these days."

"I can hear the derision in your tone from here." Wyatt laughed. Her and Hamson, they were like giggling schoolgirls sometimes, talking about him.

"How's Colchester?" asked Gray.

"We're coming to the end of the programme," said Wyatt. "Pivot is probably going to be closed down and the team dispersed."

Gray had met Wyatt when she was in Thanet as part of an investigation into the the wrongful conviction of a criminal

Gray had put away. Prior to that Wyatt had worked for CEOP, the Child Exploitation and Online Protection Command and the National Crime Agency.

"Why? Pivot has been a huge success."

"That's precisely the problem, Sol. Yarrow is in demand. He's destined for bigger and better tasks. There's word of him moving up to the Kent and Essex Serious Crime Directorate. But keep that between us, Yarrow told me in confidence."

"Good for him," said Gray. "And you can trust me to keep quiet."

"Don't get me wrong, Sol. He's done a great job. Yarrow says I'll be fine, but I don't know."

"He has a soft spot for you."

"We've been over this, Sol. Just because Adam is going through a divorce doesn't mean he's interested in me. He likes you too much to tread on your toes."

"Honourable of him."

"Sol." Gray could hear the warning in her tone.

"You can't blame me for defending my patch."

"Patch? What am I? Some piece of grass you cock your leg on and mark to keep the other dogs off?"

"Bloody hell, Em, I didn't mean that."

Gray negotiated the Clock Tower roundabout and turned up Fort Road towards Odell House, which was less than a mile away now.

He heard a sigh over the speaker. "Sorry, we've been under a lot of pressure recently. The lot we're trying to round up are particularly vicious."

"Who?"

"An Albanian gang."

"Where will you be moving next? Somewhere closer to home, I hope?" Wyatt lived in Deal, about half an hour's drive from Gray. "You always have a plan. What are you thinking?" There was a long pause on the line, enough for Gray to think the call had dropped. "Emily, are you still there?"

"I'm considering applying to Margate."

"Really? Why?"

"Isn't that obvious, Sol? We've barely seen each other for an age. Even our rare days off never overlap."

"I'm not sure Margate is a good idea."

"Don't you want everyone to know about us?"

"It's not that." Gray flicked on his indicator to turned into the station car park. "I just think with your skill set you'd be better elsewhere, like in the KESCD."

"Trying to get rid of me?"

Gray headed past Odell House and entered the car park to the rear of the building. "Not at all."

"What's the problem with us being open about their relationship? I don't understand your reluctance."

"We've been over this, Em."

"Have we?"

"I spent a long time alone before we got together. It's not easy for me."

"I understand, Sol, I really do. But I think we should be growing our relationship and we can't do that when we never see each other."

"By moving to Margate?"

"Of course. What else?"

"There has to be something better, surely?"

"Do you mean *somebody* better?"

"That's not what I said."

Wyatt cut Gray off. "Okay, I get it. Maybe you're right."

"Emily, no."

"Look, I've got to go, I've got a meeting coming up."

"Emily?" Gray pulled up in front of an empty space. "Emily?" But she'd gone. A car behind blew their horn. Gray waved an apology and he reversed into the space. Gray tried to call Wyatt but his phone rang before he could connect.

"Morning, Von," he said.

"You're late, Sol," she said. "Again."

"I'm on my way up, have the coffee waiting."

"Who's in charge here?"

"I wish I knew." Gray disconnected before Hamson could respond. He locked his car, headed into the station. He paused for a moment, rang Wyatt's number but the call dropped straight to voicemail.

"Crap," said Gray then went inside the station to meet Hamson. His relationship would once more have to wait.

Five

Halfway into Sylvia's old office Gray paused. Originally, Sylvia's desk had faced the door he'd just walked through. Here she had been the gatekeeper controlling access to Jeff Carslake, Hamson's predecessor, in a 1970s-style arrangement of secretary and boss. Hamson hadn't bothered replacing Sylvia, blaming austerity and budget cuts for the decision. But her desk was gone, only the filing cabinets lining the walls remained.

Gray knocked, a single rap before entering; his one deference to Hamson's authority. Hamson glanced over her shoulder. She was standing at the coffee machine in a corner of the room. A cup awaited Gray on the conference table opposite. Beyond was Hamson's cluttered desk in front of a large plate-glass window overlooking the road and out towards the brown sea of The English Channel. The blinds were open to maximise the light and the view. On a clear day and with some average binoculars it was possible to see the Belgian coast from here.

Gray pulled out a chair and sat. Hamson took the place across from him. "How many reminders do I have to send you for these meetings, Sol?"

"Crimes don't occur on schedule, Von, so I don't see how I can work to a routine either."

The little wrinkle appeared on Hamson's forehead just above the bridge of her nose, indicating an irritation she was trying to manage. Gray got in before Hamson did. He spread his hands, palms up. "Look, I'm aware you've been very busy and this is the only way we can catch up. I'll try to do better, okay?"

"I know you too well to fall for that one."

He decided to move the subject on. "Is Marsh still running you around?" Superintendent Bernard Marsh was Hamson's boss and based out of Maidstone.

"He's always on the bloody phone. You'd think he had nothing better to do with his time."

"You're a rising star." And she was. "You've done a great job since your promotion last year."

"We all have."

"No, Von. Sometimes you don't realise quite how much you've actually achieved. Morale was stale and we're short-handed due to all the cut backs. You've kept everybody going."

Plus there had been a strand of corruption running through Odell House after years of mismanagement, which Hamson had quietly rooted out. But Gray didn't want to mention that accomplishment out loud, it was too painful for both of them. "The crime stats are data points most DCI's would kill for. Overall, well down in pretty much every measure." Gray would be raising the spike in drug-related deaths shortly.

"If only that were all."

"I don't understand, Von."

"I think Marsh has a thing for me." Gray burst out laughing. "It's not bloody funny, Sol. He's got a wife. What is it with me and married men?"

"Is that the only problem?"

The line on Hamson's brow appeared again. A few years ago Hamson had been involved with a married colleague, Mike Fowler. Since they'd split, Hamson had remained single. "And he's at least fifteen years older than me."

"Sugar daddy, then."

"God, no. I'm not that keen on my career. Anyway, how's Emily?"

Now it was Gray's turn to feel some discomfort. He shifted in his seat. "She's fine. We're fine."

"Really." Hamson didn't sound convinced. "You're a lucky man to have her, you know."

"I spoke with Emily just before you called. She said Pivot's coming to an end."

"So I've heard. The powers that be are wanting to centralise the operation. I was briefed about the next steps yesterday at Maidstone HQ."

"Was it a private meeting with Marsh?" Gray grinned.

"Don't start, Sol. Other DCIs were there too."

"It was too easy. What was said?"

"As usual it's all rather vague, but there's a general move towards integrating the individual forces. We're too fragmented. The county forces rarely operate beyond their geographic boundaries, yet criminal gangs are becoming larger and more organised, behaving nationally and even internationally."

"That's true. It's about time we changed our methods."

"Already beginning with the KESCD, don't forget."

"Two regions isn't enough. We need to act across the whole of the UK."

"The problem is politics, though. If we merge two forces then one of the commanders loses their job. Who wants that?"

"What about the greater good?"

"We don't live in Sandford, Sol."

"Emily mentioned Yarrow may be moving to the KESCD."

"So I hear."

"What about you? Would you shift over?"

"After my job, Sol?"

Gray held his hands out towards her. "Bloody hell, that's the last thing I want. I had to be forced up to DI, remember?"

"Anybody else but you and I wouldn't believe them."

"Emily is considering a posting here."

"To Margate?"

"Yes."

"With all her ability and knowledge? Why?"

"That's what I said. We're too alike, you and I, Von."

Hamson scrunched up her face. "Now you're just being rude." She glanced at the clock on the wall.

"Can you talk to her for me?"

"I'm not getting involved in your personal life, Sol." Hamson raised her hands, palms out. "Anyway, I haven't got much longer. What's the big stuff we're handling right now?"

"Fatality from a likely drug overdose in Ramsgate this morning."

"Another one?"

"Did you know we'd had a total of nineteen now in the last six months?"

"Nineteen? That sounds well up."

"Over three times the normal rate, if that's what it can be called."

"Anything suspicious about their deaths?"

"Not that I've found so far."

"Keep me informed if you do."

"Sure." Gray shifted in his chair. "And I had a call from Sylvia."

Hamson lifted an eyebrow. "As in *our* Sylvia?" Hamson pointed a finger at the door to the PA's old domain.

"That's right."

"She contacted *you* of all people?"

"I was just as shocked, Von. She says her husband went missing yesterday. Headed off to work and didn't come back."

"She's *married*? The surprises keep coming. I always had Sylvia down as a lesbian."

"Jesus. You'd go apeshit if I said that."

"Female prerogative," shrugged Hamson. "But why you?"

"Apparently I'm tenacious. We never liked each other and that clearly hasn't changed since she left based on the conversation we've just had. But there's something weird going on."

"Like what?"

"I can't put my finger on it. It felt like Sylvia wasn't telling me the whole truth about her relationship with her husband. It's probably a case of a man walking out on his wife so I'm going to pass the case on to Worthington."

Hamson shook her head. "I'd strongly suggest not giving Sylvia's case to him."

"Seriously?"

"She'll need dealing with sensitively and that's not Worthington's forte."

"It's hardly mine either."

"Everything is comparative." Hamson cut off Gray's next response. "And before you go on, Sol, that's what I want."

"All right. If you insist." Gray would regroup, find another way to ditch the Myerscough case.

"And I need you to have words with Worthington. We've had some complaints."

"Like what?"

"Racist comments, about Jews."

"Pfeffer?"

"That's right."

"I've witnessed some of his behaviour. I'm not impressed."

"It's not Pfeffer who's raised it. Others have overheard things he's been saying and brought them to my attention. It's simply not acceptable, Sol. We're better than that. Talk to him, tell him to shut his mouth or there will be a disciplinary."

"Bloody hell. You know this isn't my kind of thing."

"Tough, you're a DI now. And besides," Hamson grinned, "I had to manage you often enough."

"Thanks."

"Joking aside, Worthington needs to get his act together. We're too short-handed for a suspension."

"Are you suggesting we let him off?"

"No, I'm bloody not! I certainly don't want him getting away with the shit he's been spouting. So, nip it in the bud please, now. It's important. Internal complaints are bad enough. I certainly don't want anything from the public."

"Your wish is my command." Gray knew when he was beaten.

"How are you finding Pfeffer?" asked Hamson.

"I've not had much contact with her, but what I've seen is very good. She'll go far, I reckon."

"And that's why I don't want to lose her because of a dick like Worthington."

"I think Pfeffer is tougher than that." Gray drained his coffee. It was lukewarm now. "What about the vacant sergeant's position? I keep getting asked." Derek Ibbotson had transferred over from the Cheshire Constabulary and been off sick pretty much ever since.

Hamson shook her head. "I'm waiting to hear if he's going to take early retirement or not."

"This has gone on for far too long, Von. He's been off ill for more days than he pretended to work here. I talked to some of his old colleagues. His management were well aware of his attendance issues. He was known as Sick Note."

"I've had words with his previous DI about keeping that fact quiet prior to the transfer, but there's nothing I can do now. We're stuck with him."

"Not for much longer, I hope? His cheesy shoes need filling."

"I've no idea, Sol." Hamson sipped her coffee. "HR-related matters are never fast. My hands are tied. Once I know, you'll know."

"We're struggling for resource."

"Nagging me won't help." Hamson went to her desk. "I'd better get on. Say hello to Emily for me. I'm jealous of her."

Gray paused, halfway up from his seat. "Why?"

Hamson laughed. "Don't have such an ego. I'm not envious because she has you."

"Oh, that's all right then." Gray got upright.

"I mean that she's got a great job, stays busy and maintains a relationship. It's not easy. I should know."

"We haven't seen much of each other recently."

"Even five minutes is longer than my last tryst."

"Are you still going to those speed dating things?"

"Speed dating? It's not the '90s anymore. Anyway," Hamson waved a hand at him. "Clear off and don't forget to deal with Worthington."

Dismissed, Gray left Hamson's office. Mission certainly not accomplished. Gray still had Sylvia's case and now a personnel problem with Worthington to manage.

Six

Gray decided it best to follow Hamson's orders for once. Usually people issues were the last items on his list to be addressed but he knew Hamson well enough that she wouldn't let this go. And Worthington's attitude was the kind which got Gray's back up.

He paused in the entrance to the Detectives' Office. Worthington wasn't at his desk, nor was he in discussion with any of his CID colleagues. Gray could see Pfeffer, however. Hamson hadn't said to speak with her; then again Hamson hadn't said not to either.

Pfeffer glanced up from her screen as Gray stood over her. She stopped tapping away at the keyboard. "Sir?"

"Have you got a moment, Melanie?"

"Of course."

"Not here."

Gray headed out of the office, paused beside the nearest unoccupied interview room. He waited just inside until Pfeffer joined him. He pointed to a chair. "Sit down, Melanie."

She did, back straight, hands in her lap. "What's wrong, sir? Have I done something?"

Gray sat opposite her. He tried to take a casual posture, one leg crossed over the other, one arm over the back of his chair. "I just want to have a quick chat." He felt awkward again.

"Okay."

How have your first few weeks gone?"

"I've really enjoyed them sir. It's actually three months and they've flown by."

"I'm glad to hear that. Normally I conduct a probation interview which I think we're a little overdue for. Just to ensure you're settling in, whether you have any concerns or difficulties. Is there anything you want to raise?"

Pfeffer shook her head slowly, her face expressionless. "Not that I can think of. All has been fine, better than I'd hoped to be honest. Everyone is nice and I appreciate being able to get on with the job without too much interference."

"It's just there have been some complaints."

Pfeffer frowned. "Complaints about me?"

"About some things that have apparently been said to you."

"Oh, I get it." Pfeffer rolled her eyes. "Regarding my beliefs, right?"

"Correct."

"It's nothing, honestly. I've had it most of my life. Actually, being a Jew is quite useful sometimes. If a member of the public accuses me of being a pig I tell them I can't eat bacon." Pfeffer grinned.

"Verbal abuse is simply unacceptable, Melanie. You shouldn't aceept or laugh about it. Particularly not from colleagues."

"I've dealt with people like DC Worthington before." Pfeffer shook her head, seeming more in frustration than anything else. "All I want to do is the best job I can, then go home, opening a bottle of wine and relaxing in front of the TV. A handful of stupid words by other people are hardly going to put me off.

I've got thick skin and if he's on at me then he's leaving others alone."

"Is Worthington saying stuff to other people in the station?"

"He's after is a promotion, sir. Everyone who's even the slightest competition is a target."

"That's how you see it?"

"Absolutely. Word is Sergeant Ibbotson isn't coming back so Worthington is keen to get the soon to be vacant spot."

Based on how Worthington had behaved yesterday with Pfeffer, Gray suspected it was more than just simple rivalry. "I'll be having a word with your colleague, as you put it."

"Sir, please, I don't want you to. Whatever he thinks and why he thinks it is deep-rooted. No disrespect, sir, but a few comments from you aren't going to change his mind. You'll just drive his opinion underground." Pfeffer appeared genuinely concerned.

"All right. I'll keep this between us."

Concern switched to relief. "Thank you, sir. Is that all?"

"Unless there's anything else you'd like to add?"

"As I said, I'm enjoying myself and I'm glad I asked for the posting. You're a good boss."

"You never see me, Melanie."

"That's what I meant, sir." Pfeffer grinned.

"Just remember, if anything becomes a problem I'm here."

"Okay, I will." Pfeffer stood and left the room.

Gray was surprised Pfeffer was willing to allow casual prejudice to continue unchecked – then again he was white, middle class, middle-aged; hardly the demographic to suffer racism. He wasn't convinced Worthington's actions were just about promotion. And clearly, neither was Pfeffer.

Pfeffer's eyes were on Gray when he entered the Detectives' Office, watching him as he crossed the room. Worthington was back at his desk on the phone. But Gray was going to pick his moment with the DC and this wasn't it.

GRAY FLEXED IN HIS chair, making the muscles in the base of his back strain. He was tired, it had been a long day but at least it was nearly over. He'd just finished interogating the PNC database for any information about Jasper Myerscough and found nothing of consequence. His mobile rang.

"Sol, it's Damian." Boughton, the beat cop, his words a rush. It was hard for Gray to hear him, sounded like he was in a wind tunnel. "Are you in the middle of anything?"

"I'm at the station," said Gray. "I was about to go home."

"You can't, not yet."

"Why?"

"Remember our conversation earlier? About the drugs supply round here?" Gray did, but failed to get the chance to say so because Boughton ploughed on. "I've got someone who'll speak to you, but he's nervous, I can't keep him here for long."

"I'm on my way. Just tell me where."

Seven

The statue of the Shell Lady stood at the end of the harbour arm, blind eyes staring out across the choppy waters off Margate. The lights of Dreamland blinked to Gray's left, in the centre stood the domineering high rise concrete slab of Arlington House and to the right the coastline meandered away in the direction of Minnis Bay where Sylvia lived.

On the bench beside the Shell Lady Gray recognised Boughton's bulk, a much smaller person beside him, leaving Gray a space at the other end. Gray sat, pulling his coat tighter about him. Though the evening was warm there a cool breeze blew off the sea.

The harbour arm was designed to protect the inner waters from bad weather, built in a time when the fishing fleet was large. Now just a couple of boats fed a single fishmongers shop on the island.

So, the harbour arm had transformed into a Bohemian extension of the nearby Old Town. There was a bar, café and several galleries displaying the wares of local artists – trying to catch some of the glow from the adjacent Turner Contemporary. But the lights of commerce didn't fall on the bench and the three of them were in increasing shadow as dusk turned to night.

The man sitting next to Boughton shrunk even further into himself with Gray's arrival, hunching over. He was thin, short and nervous, if the shakes were anything to go by. His face pale and sweaty. The man didn't acknowledge Gray. He kept his eyes fixed straight forward, focused on some point in the waves.

Boughton looked across the man's back and said, "This is Stretch." His street handle. He assumed the epithet was ironic. Boughton would for sure know his real name and tell Gray later. For now Stretch would do, anything to make him feel more comfortable. Boughton said to Stretch, "Sol is all right."

"Okay," said Stretch.

"Hello," said Gray.

"Stretch knows everything and everybody," said Boughton.

"That's right." Stretch straightened slightly, perhaps a normal habit to puff out his chest, to seem important. He smoothed his wild hair down with one hand. "Who you asking about?"

"A guy called Lippy," said Gray.

"I knew him. He weren't no friend, but yeah, the poor bastard."

"Is there anything you can tell me about Lippy?"

"Talked far too much, that's how he got his name, course. Once he started it was hard to shut him up." Stretch rolled his eyes. "Mind you, I'd heard he was clean so I was surprised he OD'd." He shrugged. "Must have had a relapse, maybe his body couldn't take it. Won't be the last."

"That's why I wanted to talk with you. About the overdoses."

Stretch eyed Gray. "It's been going on for years. Why are you bothered now?"

"We're seeing a lot more deaths."

"Just a few junkies didn't matter?"

"That's not what I meant."

"Fucking cops." Stretch nudged his chin towards Gray. "You pretend to care, is all."

"I'm here because I want to help," said Gray. "People are dying."

"Don't you think I know that?" Stretch ran fingers through his hair. "Christ, I moved to Margate to get away from shit like this."

"How long have you lived here?" asked Boughton.

"Just over a year. I'm from Wythenshawe."

"Manchester, right?"

"Yeah, man." Gray caught Stretch's grin.

"City or United?"

"United?" Stretch spat on the floor. "A Blue to the end, pal."

"I'm a Charlton man myself."

"That's crap."

"Can't help where you're born, right?"

"True enough."

Football, thought Gray. *The great leveller.*

"So," said Boughton, "you moved here last year?"

"Right," nodded Stretch. "And it was great at first. By the sea, family didn't know where I was, good supply of gear, a bit of busking to raise some cash. Got some mates. Even the squat was all right." He sighed. "Until it changed."

"How?"

"My supply dried up. I hurt like hell while I was coming down. But then it returned." Stretch leant his head back briefly, like raindrops were falling on his contented face. "I can't tell you how good that was. Man, it were wonderful. The stuff was better, cheaper too."

"When was this?"

"It was cold. January, I suppose."

Which was the time when the Pivot operation had swept up the local dealer network.

"Go on, Stretch," said Boughton.

"That's when things weren't the same no more. After a few weeks of the new stuff the price for a wrap began to creep up. I was told I could only buy from one dealer. Before, I had four dealers, but that stopped. If I went to anyone else they refused to sell."

"Why?"

"People started developing trust issues, and there was some new guy hanging in the background, always watching. My dealer got tough on me. Stuff happened."

"Like what, Dean?" asked Boughton, his voice lower. Gray picked up on the PC's use of Stretch's real name.

Stretch shifted his stance, like he had an itch. "E, my dealer, weren't no friend no more. She seemed scared herself." Stretch fell silent, the waves beat against the harbour arm beneath their feet a couple of times while Stretch thought. "Yeah, scared. That's what we all are now. But what can you do? You gotta have the stuff, you know? Stretch glanced around. "But I'm all right now, I'm off the junk."

Maybe that was why Stretch was shaking – withdrawal symptoms.

"There's a new gang what's taken over," said Stretch. "Using the guys who was on the street dealing before the other lot went. This bunch, they're hard. You don't mess Albanians around."

"They run things now?" asked Gray. He remembered Wyatt mentioning an Albanian gang she was tackling.

"That's right. They're weird, man. They work like terrorists, in cells. E, she only knows the bloke above him and so on. She hates it. And there's no grassing neither or working with the cops, 'cos if you do or they even suspect it the next score you make it's a blowout and you're done. One last happy trip while your brain explodes." He shuddered. "Several of my mates have gone like that. It's why I gave up. I'm safe now. Others have been beaten up or their girlfriends or sisters raped if they feel you're out of order and need teaching a lesson."

"Jesus," said Boughton.

"He won't help me, you or anyone else," said Stretch.

"How many rapes have there been?" asked Gray.

"Dunno, several."

"I haven't heard of this happening."

Stretch snorted. "Course not. If it got reported things would be much worse next time."

"What's E's full name?"

Stretch goggled at Gray. "No way. I've already told you far too much. I don't want no kicking."

"I want to help."

"It's too risky." Stretch shook his head. "And you can't do shit."

"Tell me the name of your dealer."

"No way!"

"If you don't I'll get word out that you've been speaking with us."

"Sol," said Boughton. Gray ignored him.

"It's only a kicking, right Dean? I'll bet you've taken a few of those before."

"You bastard," said Stretch, clenching and unclenching his hands.

"All I need is a name and I promise, you'll never hear from me again."

Stretch stared at Gray for a long, long moment, his jaw working, like he was chewing gum but he was talking quietly to himself.

"Okay," said Gray. "If you won't give me anything I'm not wasting any more of my time." He stood. "Don't say you weren't warned." He began to walk away and heard urgent footsteps behind him. Stretch grabbed his arm, stopped him.

"Petrela," said Stretch. "Her surname's Petrela."

"What's E short for?"

"Dunno. She's never said." Stretch was really sullen now.

"Thank you," said Gray.

"Piss off," said Stretch. He turned to Boughton. "Don't come near me again." He shoved his hands in his pockets and walked away fast. Gray sat back down next to Boughton.

"Was that really necessary?" asked Boughton.

"Stretch wasn't going to talk otherwise."

"He might have eventually."

"*Might* and *eventually* aren't good enough, Damian. From what Stretch was saying there's a gang out there abusing and murdering people. I want to find them and put a stop to it."

"Even if it means putting someone at risk?"

"Nothing will happen to him. He's off the gear, said so himself. And who's going to tell him we've been speaking?"

"I hope you're right, Sol."

"What's Stretch's full name, by the way?"

"Dean Mold."

"And do you know this dealer of his, Petrela?"

"She operates over on Godwin Road by the synagogue." Boughton hiked a thumb over his shoulder, Cliftonville way. He stood. "Please don't make me regret reaching out to you."

"Damian, you know I'm right. If people are suffering we have to get to the bottom of what's happening, relationships be damned."

Boughton stared at him for a long moment before he followed in Stretch's footsteps, leaving Gray to contemplate the dark waves.

GRAY HEADED BACK TO Odell House, walking fast up the incline of Fort Road, past the Turner Contemporary. It was well beyond the end of his shift, but it wasn't like he had anything else to do. He'd never had many close friends, and after his wife's suicide over a decade ago, most of his acquaintances had slunk away. Only a couple of people stuck by him.

He entered through the front, raised a hand at the tubby, moustachioed Sergeant Morgan on the desk, who let him through the security door and into the station's bowels.

The Detectives' Office was sparsely populated. Once it had buzzed with activity, but now, in these times of austerity cutbacks were biting hard. Yet the criminals were stronger than ever while it seemed the detectives available to Gray were fewer than they used to be. Hardly anyone wanted to join up.

Gray sat at his desk, accessed the PNC and typed in Stretch's real name – 'Dean Mold'. The system gave him several possibilities. He clicked on one after the other until he the right record. Stretch was twenty-seven, a litany of minor crimes to his credit. Mancunian as he'd said. An address on Norfolk Road in Cliftonville, not far from where Petrela worked.

Then he looked for Petrela herself. Turned out the E stood for Emina. She'd been arrested for possession of a wrap, given a caution and released. Looking at Petrela's scowling mug shot Gray reckoned all Petrela delivered was trouble and pain.

She had tattoos on her face and neck. A prominent swirl of roses around her throat, a line of tears running down from one eye and a 'swirl' above her eyebrow. Her hair was tied back. A side shot showed her hair was shaved – an inch wide section above her ear – and more tattoos there. There was hardly any personal information listed. Only that she was from Kukes in Albania and was twenty years old.

Gray sat back and focused on her face. Nineteen deaths. He was going to pay Petrela a visit and find out what the hell was going on.

Eight

"Still here, Sol?" Hamson, standing in his doorway. She wore a smart red coat, a tiny handbag slung over one shoulder rather than the laptop case she usually carried everywhere. "Anybody would think you'd got nothing better to do."

"That's me, the centre of everyone's universe."

"I was going to head home, open a bottle of wine. Want to join me?"

"At your house?"

"I'm joking, you idiot. If you want a quick drink though, I could do with one. Next door at The Britannia?"

"I was about to head somewhere." Godwin road, specifically.

"Please," said Hamson. "I could do with the company."

Maybe Petrela could wait a little. "As long as you're paying." Hamson didn't say no. "There's somewhere else far better than The Britannia I can think of."

"CHRIST, SOL, THIS PLACE is a dive," said Hamson as she sat and slid a pint glass across the table. "And the guy behind the bar almost fell over when I dared ask for wine." Hamson had a pint herself, so clearly the answer to Hamson's question had been 'No'. She kept her coat on, buttoned up.

PITY THE DEAD

Gray wasn't surprised the landlord of The English Flag in the Old Town, a balding lowlife called Dick, hadn't given him the full measure. It was Dick's way of thumbing his nose at authority.

The pub seemed to be always open. It was a grubby melting pot of xenophobia, the George Cross hanging behind the way a clear indication of how the regulars felt. This was the last corner for the disaffected in the increasingly upmarket Old Town.

"I quite like it," said Gray.

"Really? It's obvious everyone knows what we are, given the looks we're getting."

"Think of it as local colour."

"Blood red if this lot had their way."

"It's you they're glaring at, not me. You're a woman."

"God, can it get any worse?" Hamson drank her lager.

"What did you want to talk about?" asked Gray.

"Nothing work related, it's just we don't see each other very much these days."

"We have regular meetings, Von."

"They don't count." Hamson downed some more of her drink. "Actually, I'm going out shortly and I need some Dutch courage."

"When are you going home to get yourself ready?"

"I already am, you cheeky bugger." Hamson undid her coat, revealing a printed floral dress.

"Who's the lucky guy?"

"Nobody you know, thankfully."

"That's a shame."

"And kind of my point."

"I hope you've checked him out on the PNC to make sure he's not got a record and married," said Gray. Straightaway he realised he'd gone too far and Hamson's acid glare was confirmation. A reminder of Mike Fowler once more.

"You really know how to pour cold water on a promising situation, Sol."

"Sorry. It was meant as a joke. I hope it goes well."

"Gee, thanks." Hamson drank some more of her lager.

"Where are you meeting?"

"So you can leer in through the windows and pull faces?"

Gray raised his hands in surrender. "Genuine question."

She shook her head. "It's all right. I'm just wired. It's been a while." She had another drink. "Have you talked to Worthington yet?"

"I thought this was supposed to be a non-work related conversation?"

"I need some normality. As you said, go with it. So, have you?"

"I've not had the chance."

"It needs doing."

"I know. I had a chat with Pfeffer, though. She reckons Jerry wants the sergeant's role and he sees Pfeffer as competition."

"That's bullshit."

"Maybe."

"Definitely."

"I plan to go over all this with him, don't worry," said Gray. Hamson checked her watch. "Time to go?"

"Another few minutes. We're meeting across the road at the bistro. And it wouldn't do to be early."

"Speaking of talking, I met an ex-junkie called Stretch earlier."

"Sounds just as much fun as being in here."

"This guy reckons a new supplier has moved into the area."

"Well, we knew that. The users have to be getting their gear from somewhere."

"He mentioned Albanians. Apparently they're brutal in how they operate – they use the threat of violence and rape to keep everyone in order."

"Rape?" Hamson shuddered.

"And Stretch reckoned some of his junkie mates are being murdered if the dealer thinks they've been talking to the cops. They're given a hot hit. What we see is a spike in the death rate but who cares about an overdose? We record it as an accidental death and move on."

"And overdoses are up over three hundred per cent, you said."

"Correct."

"Good God, why has this not come to our attention before now?"

"Because they're all scared and we weren't paying attention."

Gray kept back that Boughton had already made mention of the deaths to Worthington. He'd deal with the DC on that as well. If senior management learned what had been ignored there would be a significant problem for Gray and Hamson.

"Chillingly effective."

"Isn't it?" Gray downed some of his pint, his throat suddenly dry.

"Marsh probably won't be happy."

"Why would you tell him, Von?"

Hamson gave Gray a puzzled look. "Are you seriously asking *why* I'd keep my boss informed of major matters, Sol? I'd expect the same of you."

"All I'm saying is that now might not be the time to be talking to him. We don't have all the answers, just lots of questions and you know what the superintendent is like. My advice is let me get a bit further along before you bring Marsh up to speed."

Hamson thought briefly. "Keep me informed as you move forward. Let's discuss each stage, okay?"

"Works for me."

Hamson put her glass down slowly then span it ninety degrees. Eventually she said, "Actually there is something else we need to cover. There's been a complaint. About you."

"Wouldn't be the first time."

"Oh, but this one is."

Gray sat back, crossed his arms. "Go on."

"Inappropriate behaviour with DC Pfeffer."

Gray laughed. Hamson didn't. "Seriously?" asked Gray.

"One hundred per cent, Sol."

"Good God, that's ridiculous. She's half my age."

"Less than half, actually."

"Bloody hell. Talk about rubbing vinegar in the cut." Gray leaned forward. "Who complained? Was it Worthington?"

"Why him?"

"Just gut instinct."

"It was Worthington." Hamson shook her head. "I shouldn't even be telling you this."

"Why are you?"

"Because I want you to watch your back. I can't go another man down, we're too thin on the ground as it is."

"That's all?"

Hamson frowned. "Of course, why would it be anything else?" She checked her watch. "I'd better go. He'll be waiting." She finished her pint. As they left Gray gave the landlord a cheery wave and received a scowl in response.

When they were outside Hamson said, "You know before you told me about junkies overdosing the only thought on my mind was, what if my date doesn't like me? Now that seems rather trite."

"Of course he'll like you. If not then he's a fool, tell him so and try again. Main thing is you're doing something with someone who's not a cop."

"Do you really believe that?"

"Yes, Von." He gave Hamson a kiss on the cheek. "Good luck. Text me later to tell me how it went."

Hamson put her hand to where Gray's lips had touched. "Will do," she said.

Gray walked back to the station to pick up his car. He might have played down his feelings to Hamson but Gray was angry. Worthington's complaint was pure office politics and crude at that.

But he wasn't planning on going straight home, because he had a visit to make.

GRAY WATCHED PETRELA in his driver's side mirror. She was right where Boughton had said she'd be. He'd parked on Albion Road near the intersection with Godwin Road. Godwin Road connected the major thoroughfares of the Eastern Esplanade, which tracked along the coast and past Odell House, not quite a mile away, and Northdown Road which was the main commercial area of Cliftonville – what had once been an upmarket conurbation.

The car faced up the road in shadow and Gray hunched down in his seat so she wouldn't see his face. Petrela, on the other hand, stood right out in the open. Leaning against a rusting slatted metal fence, beneath one of the few working street lamps.

Behind Petrela was a large brick building, the sharply angled roof in the style of a church, the windows covering a narrow metal grille, clearly designed to stop the glass being smashed. The synagogue. Pfeffer might even worship there.

Gray figured this was a good location to do business. With a turn of her head, Petrela had excellent visibility of all the approaches to her. From what Stretch had said, Petrela only dealt with people she knew. And she wore gloves, no fingerprints to pass on.

One lesson Gray had learned from his time on Pivot; Petrela was likely to be carrying very little product on her; probably some cocaine, maybe some Spice, a synthetic drug designed to mimic marijuana. There was an extensive homeless community in Thanet and in the last year or so Spice had become their escapism of choice. Petrela would have a drug stash nearby, somewhere she could head back to and collect more of what she needed.

Just then she pushed off and stood upright. She had a customer. The pair embraced in a hug. There was some patting on the back with one hand, the other obscured between their bodies. Gray would place a bet which no other cop would take that an exchange going on between them. A folded note in return for a wrap.

After a few moments they parted, transaction complete. Petrela regained her position, ignoring her customer who was walking fast towards Gray. As he neared, Gray recognised him.

Stretch.

So he'd lied.

Gray ducked further down in his seat and twisted his head away, not wanting to be seen. But Stretch was too intent on getting to wherever he was going as quickly as possible, presumably home for a hit.

Someone else approached Petrela moments later, moving in a shambling gait, twitchy and hunched over. A hood pulled over their face, so Gray wasn't sure if they were a man or a woman. The transactional process was identical; another hug. They clasped briefly, then the shambler moved away, faster. Petrela returned to leaning against the fence, hands in pockets.

Gray got out of his car. Once, when he'd been on the beat he had attempted to buy some drugs from a local dealer. He'd succeeded and the guy had gone down for it. But that was years ago when he had the confidence of youth and dealers weren't as savvy. Gray walked towards Petrela, not really sure how to open the conversation. She eyed him all the way, her expression flat, emotionless.

He paused a couple of feet away. "All right," he said. Petrela just stared at him. He tried again. "I'm after something."

"Like what?" asked Petrela, her accented tone as lifeless as her features. "Directions? A blow job?"

"You know, a bit of gear."

Petrela shrugged. "No idea what you're on about, man."

"I was told you'd be able to help me."

"I can't do nothing for you."

"Are you sure? My friend was explicit."

"Then where is he? Your friend."

"At home."

"Sure."

"I've been asking around, trying to get some help, but nobody will. You're my last chance. I need something."

"I don't know who you are or what you want. Bring your *mate* and maybe I'll point you in the right direction, or don't come back."

"I'm desperate."

"Then you'd better get a move on." Petrela leant back on the fence. He'd been dismissed. He got back into his car. He would get Stretch to vouch for him, but by now he'd bet Stretch would probably be off his face on the drugs he'd just bought from Petrela.

When Gray drove away he saw Petrela in his rearview staring after him. She was sharp, intelligent. By no means your average drone on the street making fast cash and without any perception of the implications of their actions. She and her organisation needed dealing with.

Jasper Myerscough hardly seemed important in comparison to a swath of deaths.

Nine

Gray lived in an apartment block just back from the chalky cliffs on the Broadstairs sea front, between the main horseshoe shaped Viking Bay and the smaller, less-frequented Louisa Bay. He paused for the gates to the underground car park to slide open. Headlights illuminated a portion of the poorly lit cavity. His allotted space was roughly central. Gray nudged his car into the spot, turned the engine off and the lights died. He started walking towards the far wall for the lift, threading his way between other vehicles.

As he neared the lift he heard quick steps behind him. He began to turn and caught a glimpse of a person running at him before he was struck. He barrelled forwards, hitting the concrete floor hard, barely having the time to throw out his hands to break his fall. The breath whooshed out of his lungs. A pair of knees pushed hard into his back. He bucked but a hand grabbed his hair, pushed his head down, pressing his nose into the concrete. Then his right arm was yanked up until the tendons began to scream. He yelped in pain. He was pinned tight.

Some of the pressure on his arm released and he felt the person swivel on his spine as they leaned forward. Something was pushed into his mouth, making him gag. He clamped his teeth down. The weight came off him and his arm released. He started to move but then he was hit on the head and all went completely dark.

GRAY COULD HEAR SOMEBODY speaking, but a buzzing buried the words. As he rose from a deep hole and clawed his way to consciousness his skull felt like it was being hammered. He could smell rubber and oil. He opened his eyes, and immediately closed them again because it hurt. He coughed, something in his mouth. He spat out whatever it was.

Less of the buzzing now.

"Are you all right?" a woman's voice.

Gray opened his eyes once more and saw a pair of red high heeled shoes. He groaned, rolled over and tried to sit up. Hands helped him, pulling on his arms. He winced, pain where his attacker had stretched tendons. He sat, hunched over, head hung, feeling like he wanted to be sick. He waited to let the sensation pass. His palms began to sting now. He'd skinned them when he hit the floor. His knees too, trousers shredded.

"What happened?" asked the woman. She squatted down, staring at him, concern etched across her features. Gray assumed she was another resident in the block, because what other reason did she have to be down here? Or maybe a visitor, because he didn't recognise her. She was middle-aged, short dark hair, large brown eyes.

"I fell over," said Gray. "Banged my head." There was a piece of scrunched-up paper beside him. It must have been what he'd spat out of his mouth. He grabbed it.

He struggled to his feet, the woman doing her best to help him, and shoved the paper into his pocket. "I'll be okay." Finally upright, he swayed as his world span round. He waited again, then began to walk towards the lift, the woman under his shoulder, supporting him. She pressed the up arrow. The lift descended, the doors opened and they shuffled inside.

"What floor are you on?" she asked.

"Four."

She thumbed the button and the lift jerked upwards. Bile rose in Gray's throat with the motion. Thankfully soon the lift drew to a halt and let them out. "Which way?" she asked. He pointed.

"Here," he said when they reached his front door. He fished around in his pocket for his keys. She took them from him and led him inside. "I'll be fine now, thanks."

"If you're sure."

Gray nodded, making his head hurt. "Thanks for your help."

"I'm Angela," she said. "I'm on the floor above." She fished around in her handbag, pulled out a business card. "I'll leave this here." She put the card on the coffee table. "Call me if I can do anything. I'll see myself out."

Once she'd gone, Gray headed to his drinks cabinet, got a bottle of brandy and a glass, poured himself a large shot and downed it. The alcohol hit his stomach, made it lurch again. He ran into the bathroom, leaned over the toilet and threw up.

When there was nothing left to evacuate, he righted himself. He felt grubby. He turned on the shower. While the water heated up, he slowly stripped off, throwing his clothes in a pile. He got under the jets, leant against the wall, hissed when the water hit painful parts. Carefully he washed grit out of the cuts and scrapes. He stayed in the shower until he felt a little better. Eventually he stepped out, the room full of steam despite the extractor fan powering away overhead.

Gray towelled himself dry. He went to the sink, wiped a hand across the mirror and inspected his face. No marks. He twisted, looked at his back. The skin was red just beneath his shoulder blades, where the man had pressed down. Pulling on a dressing gown, he went into the kitchen, made himself some tea and took the cup onto the balcony.

Then he remembered the piece of paper he'd picked up off the garage floor. He returned to the bathroom, went through the trouser pockets. The paper was damp and crushed. He unfolded it. The words had been produced with a printer, no handwriting to analyse:

Stop the investigation or it'll go bad for you.

Which one, though? He had multiple cases under his control.

Thinking about it made his head hurt.

Ten

The address was a tall, narrow terrace on Norfolk Road, two streets over from Petrela's patch in Cliftonville. Stretch's place was a dingy house on a dingy road, blackened from exhaust fumes. Gray got out of his car slowly, still aching from last night, though the Ibuprofen he'd taken this morning were helping.

The front garden was a narrow strip of mud filled with large plastic dustbins, two for each flat; household waste and recycling. Too many for the space. They spilled out onto the pavement.

Six doorbells were screwed to the wall by the entrance. This was low-rent accommodation. No video screen for the occupant to view the visitor like at Gray's. He pressed the bell for a few seconds. Nobody answered. Tried a couple more times. Zero response. He hammered on the door, then rapped on the downstairs bay window, a crack across the glass.

Finally, he heard somebody inside, fiddling with the lock. The door swung open. A woman with long grey tousled hair, clad in baggy black jogging bottoms and an even baggier t-shirt, stood there. "You woke me up," she said, her voice thick with sleep.

"Sorry," said Gray. He showed his warrant card. The yawn she was halfway through snapped off. "It's one of your neighbours I want to speak with, but he isn't answering."

She stepped out of the way. "You had me worried for a minute."

The hall was gloomy; a bike crammed under the stairs next to a stroller. The muted sound of a baby wailing came from somewhere above.

Gray said, "I'll let you get back to bed."

The woman nodded, re-entered her flat, closed him out.

He headed up the stairs, most of the steps creaking. The walls were damp to his touch and the bannister loose and rickety. As he reached Stretch's floor the baby stopped crying. He hammered on the door. It opened. In the entrance was Stretch in boxer shorts and a vest. He tried to push the door closed when recognition struck. Gray shouldered his way in, making Stretch stagger into the hallway.

"What do you want?" asked Stretch, pressed back against the wall.

"Get dressed, you're coming with me."

"Why?"

"Because I said so."

"What do you want?"

"You're going to vouch for me."

"Eh?"

"With your dealer."

Stretch backed along the corridor. "No way!"

"It's that or prison."

"Bullshit."

"I saw you, with Petrela yesterday," said Gray. A look of surprise hit Stretch's face. Caught out. "If I search your flat I reckon I'll come across something that'll get you a sentence." Gray had no idea if that were true, but it was a reasonable guess.

"If they find out, I'm in deep shit."

"They won't. All I want to do is buy some drugs."

"That's it?"

"Yes," lied Gray. "As far as Petrela is concerned, I'm just another user."

"After this you'll leave me alone?"

"We'll never see each other again, I promise."

Stretch stared at Gray, thinking, then said, "That's what you said last time."

Gray pulled out his wallet, extracted two twenty-pound notes. Stretch eyed the money, licked his lips. "Not enough."

Gray pulled out another twenty. "This is all you're getting. Take it or leave it." Stretch reached out for the cash but Gray withdrew his hand. "After, not before."

"All right," said Stretch and made his way towards the door.

"You might want to put some clothes on first."

Stretched glanced down at his bare legs, grinned. "Yeah, right, of course." He headed down the corridor to the first open doorway, went inside. Gray stayed where he was and waited. A minute later, Stretch was back. He'd pulled on jeans and a hoodie. He held a pair of red trainers in his hand, which he put on, wobbling as he did so.

"Ready?" said Gray.

Stretch nodded.

Outside they got walking, Stretch in front, Gray behind. Stretch didn't say a word and Gray left it like that. As they neared Petrela, she caught sight of them. She stood tall, ready.

Stretch stopped in his tracks, turned to Gray. "I want the money now."

"When we're done," said Gray.

"No, *now*." Stretch put out his hand. "I'm not hanging around. As soon as you two are talking, I'm gone."

Gray passed over the cash. Stretch shoved his payment into a pocket.

"This is your friend?" she asked of Gray when they were a few feet away.

"Stretch and me have known each other for years," said Gray.

Petrela turned to Stretch. "That true?"

"He's all right." Stretch nodded. "You can trust him, E."

"What are you after?" asked Petrela. Stretch stuck to his word. He walked away as fast as he could, not looking back.

"Coke," said Gray.

"Come here in an hour. I'll make sure you're sorted out."

"I can't get it now?"

"Return in an hour or don't. Your call."

GRAY'S PHONE RANG AS he was getting into his car: Clough, the Thanet pathologist. "Morning, Ben. How's things?"

"Better for me than Mr Nolan, Sol." Clough meant the junkie who'd died beneath the Ramsgate cliffs the other day. "I've carried out the PM and I've emailed you the report."

"What was your assessment?"

"Clear signs of longterm drug use, although I'd say he'd been off them for a while. His body wasn't *quite* as ravaged as others I've seen in the past. Indications are that, as I initially suspected; cause of death was an overdose."

"When will you receive the tox report?"

"I haven't asked for one."

"Why not?"

"Because of that political initiative called austerity. I don't request a toxicological analysis unless the cause of death is unclear."

"Since when?"

"Six months or more. DCI Hamson knows all about it. In fact, she required the change to be made."

"First I've heard of it."

"Then I suggest you take it up with your DCI."

"I will. Thanks for the call, Ben."

"Any time." Clough disconnected.

Gray's phone rang immediately. Hamson. "Sol, where are you?"

"Cliftonville. What's up? Have I forgotten one of our meetings again?"

"I need to see you in my office, now."

"Why?"

"Sylvia Myerscough is why."

Gray groaned.

Eleven

Neither Hamson or Sylvia appeared pleased to see Gray, which was nothing new. Sylvia, handbag on her lap, coat wrapped around her, glared at him. Hamson just seemed pissed to be in this situation.

"Party started without me?" asked Gray.

Sylvia huffed. "And this," she said, "is exactly why I'm talking to you, DCI Hamson. Solomon was at best flippant with me when I worked here. My husband is missing and nobody seems to be doing anything about it."

"I didn't want your case in the first place."

She opened her mouth to argue, but Hamson stood, raised her hands, palms out, like she was pushing the brewing argument away. "Please, squabbling isn't going to achieve anything."

"You make me sound like a child, DCI Hamson," said Sylvia.

"Well, if the cap fits," shrugged Gray, eliciting a glare from both women.

"Sit down, Sol. And Sylvia, please call me Yvonne."

Gray put himself a space away from Sylvia, facing Hamson. He crossed his arms, sat back, well aware how defensive his posture was.

"Sylvia is concerned that the investigation to find her husband isn't progressing," said Hamson.

"I'm working on it," said Gray.

"What have you done so far?" Sylvia rapped the table with a knuckle.

"I'm planning to visit your husband's employer," said Gray.

"Planning? So you haven't been yet?"

"I've organised to go today," lied Gray.

"What else?" asked Hamson.

"I've checked the PNC, nothing there, and logged the case on MisPers, no hits on that either. No reports of any sightings. So far, I've drawn a complete blank. I need something to go on, which I don't have yet."

"Have you heard from Jasper at all?" asked Hamson.

"Not a word," said Sylvia. "It's most unlike him. I'm extremely worried."

"I'm doing my best, Sylvia," lied Gray for a second time.

"I shouldn't have come in." Sylvia stood. "I know how busy you are. I apologise for disturbing you. I'll leave you alone."

Now Gray felt guilty. He didn't like Sylvia, but not enough to want to see her suffer.

"I'll show you out," said Gray.

"There's no need. I know my way." Sylvia gave him a thin smile. She nodded at Hamson. "Chief Inspector."

Once Sylvia was gone Hamson said, "Good God, could you have been any more infantile?"

"Sorry, she's always managed to get under my skin. Old habits, I guess."

"Give me an update after the visit, all right?"

"Why all the attention? Sylvia used to work here, but even so."

"She threatened to speak with Marsh."

"And? Just because Sylvia barks we all have to jump? Frankly, I've far more important cases to work on, like the drug deaths. This will be a husband walking out on his wife, you mark my words. And I wouldn't blame him either."

"You're giving me a headache."

"It's a talent," said Gray. Hamson snorted. "I was talking to Ben Clough earlier, about Nolan."

"The corpse from the Ramsgate shelters?"

"Right, Clough said it's an overdose."

"Another one then, as expected."

"He also said he wasn't going to run a tox report. On your orders. That you've a general embargo on analyses."

"That's correct. Marsh demanded further savings to our budget. This is one of them."

"I wasn't aware."

"I sent an email round."

"I didn't receive it."

Hamson raised an unimpressed eyebrow. She returned to her desk, collected her laptop, retook her place and focused briefly on the screen, clicked the built-in mouse several times. "There," she said after a few moments, turning round the laptop for him to be able to see the screen.

She had an email open, titled 'Budget Constraints'. Beneath was a brief message, stating exactly what Hamson had just said – that due to financial issues there had to be certain restrictions proposed. Analyses was one of them.

"And you got a copy." Hamson tapped the screen with a fingernail. "In fact, you're first on the list."

"I missed this somehow."

"Shall I take that as an apology?"

"There's something bothering me about all these deaths recently."

"Like what?"

"I can't put my finger on it, Von. I'd like to run some tests, see if the tox reports bring anything back."

"How many are we talking about?"

"Nineteen."

"Jesus, Sol. That'll cost thousands!" Hamson shook her head. "I assume Dr Clough has written reports and drawn conclusions on each?"

"He has."

"And, knowing Clough, the inferences as to cause are well supported?"

"They are."

"I need a clear justification from you to draw doubt on Clough's decision making."

"I can't give you anything firm right now." Gray knew that Clough would hate being questioned too.

"Then I'm unable approve the work. Bring me a defensible reason and of course we'll do what's necessary. Until you can convince me otherwise I'm afraid there will be no go-ahead from me."

"You're making a mistake, Von."

Hamson's face darkened. A red flush crept up her throat. Gray knew he'd gone too far, but he didn't feel any regret. He was right. "Sometimes you forget, DI Gray, that there's a chain of command at work. Give me what I've asked for and you may get what you want." Gray opened his mouth to argue. "Enough, inspector. The way out is over there." Hamson pointed to the door, and returned to her desk.

"Yes, ma'am." He tugged his forelock, closed the door before Hamson could swear at him. He paused at the top of the stairs, dug out his mobile and called Clough.

"I've just spoken with Hamson. She's fine to go ahead with the analyses."

"I'll need that in writing."

"You'll receive email in a few minutes."

"When I do I'll place the request."

"Thanks, Ben." Gray disconnected and returned to his office. He sat at his desk. There was a lukewarm cup of coffee that someone had put there earlier, presumably in time for his arrival. Underneath the mug was a strip of yellow paper, a post-it note. Gray lifted the mug. Written on the paper was 'Morning!', a smiley face and 'M'.

Pfeffer.

Gray rattled out a brief missive to Clough, confirming what he wanted the pathologist to do. As his finger hovered over the mouse, the arrow on 'Send', Gray considered briefly what his email might trigger and how pissed Hamson would be. But he squashed the thought and clicked the button.

Gray checked the time. Nearly half an hour before he was to be back on Godwin Road. He headed to the makeshift kitchen, getting a smile from Pfeffer as he passed by, and zapped the coffee in the microwave before returning to his seat.

The police had access to CCTV provided by the local district council. The cameras were arranged in a line along the seafront of the three towns – Ramsgate, Margate and Broadstairs – the tourist traps. The elected officials keen to keep the paying visitors safe and content. One camera was located at the bottom of West Cliff Road where Gray lived although the lens was a good few hundred yards from the turning into the car park.

Gray soon had the live feed up on his screen. There were three perspectives – both ways along the cliff path and another up West Cliff Road. A dog off its leash passed from left to right, its owner a few feet behind. A car drove down West Cliff Road.

He accessed the recorded file and wound back to the approximate time he arrived at his flat. Day retreated into night. Eventually, he caught sight of headlights coming down the road, a glare in the centre of the screen. They were his. He hadn't indicated to pull into the car park. A few seconds pause while the gate opened and then his car disappeared.

He almost missed it.

He had to zoom in, the image pixelating, but somebody detached themselves from the shadows across the road and ran over once Gray was inside. They must have got through just as the gates were closing. Gray would only have seen them at the time if he looked in his rearview, likely a brief silhouette in the entrance. But he hadn't paid any attention, too intent on getting parked.

There was no way Gray was able to get an identity from this. The only conclusion he could draw was the person appeared large enough to probably be a man, which he already knew. The clock in the bottom corner of his computer screen told him there was just under a quarter of an hour before he needed to be back on Godwin Road.

One more thing to do first. After finding the phone number for Langham's Freight & Haulage he rang them and introduced himself.

"I'd like to speak with somebody about one of your employees, Jasper Myerscough," said Gray.

"I'll put you through to our chairman, sir," said the receptionist, then she was gone.

"Andrew Langham." A baritone voice, business-like tone. "What can I do to help?"

"I've some questions about Jasper Myerscough."

"Fire away!"

"I'd prefer to ask them face to face, if that's okay."

"I'm sure I can fit you in, Inspector Gray. This morning suit you?"

"Fine."

"Just ask for me when you arrive."

Gray disconnected. He dashed out of Odell House, drove back to where Petrela worked, but her space was empty. She wasn't waiting for him after all, just some kid Gray didn't recognise, leaning against a lamp post a few yards away, fiddling with his phone.

Gray paced up and down the pavement until well after the due time. Back in his car he swore and banged his steering wheel, not paying any attention to the kid across the road.

Twelve

Gray took the A256 out of Thanet, heading south towards Dover. The dual carriageway ran past the ever-shrinking site of what was once a major pharmaceutical company outside Sandwich, the walled town itself a past glory; a now silted-up port. The surrounding area had been hit hard by the decimation of the company – many other businesses had depended on it. In all, thousands had lost their jobs, rippling out like the destructive waves after the bombshell news.

The A256 tracked through flat land, reclaimed from the sea, bypassing other industries that had come and gone. The power station at Richborough – the towers demolished years ago. And the colliery at Betteshanger – the pit filled and the slag heaps a nature reserve and cycle park. Industry and employment steadily being whittled away in this out-of-the-way corner of the country.

Overall, the drive took just under thirty minutes. Langham's was based a mile or so north of Dover, between Temple Ewell and the busy port. To the south east the imposing hulk of Dover Castle occupied the high ground and had played a major part in the local area's history over centuries. From there the escape from Dunkirk had been planned and managed in 1940 during Operation Dynamo. A few of the Little Ships which had streamed out over the channel to pick up the Allied troops still existed – one was moored in Ramsgate harbour and remained a minor tourist attraction.

Langham's itself occupied a section of flat ground off the A road. Gray drove past a large area where multiple trailers, minus their cabs, were parked up and waiting, their livery visible. Beyond Gray turned onto an unnamed road. The lorry park was to one side, the other a two storey brown brick building overlooking the vehicles. He pulled into a visitor's space right by the entrance. He introduced himself at reception and Andrew Langham stepped out of a side door almost immediately.

The chairman shook hands with Gray, his grip tight. "Pleased to meet you, Inspector Gray." Langham was a big man, powerful, smartly dressed, business casual. Chinos, a crisp white shirt and patent leather shoes. A ring of silver hair ran round the otherwise bald dome of his pâte above a broken nose which had been reset badly. Gray wouldn't be surprised if Langham was once a trucker.

He led Gray into a room just off reception, a generic meeting space. A pot of coffee and two cups with milk and sugar were already in the centre of a round table. Framed photos of trucks hung on the walls. Gray refused a drink and waited while Langham poured one for himself.

"Thank you for seeing me," said Gray.

"Not at all."

"What do you do here?"

"We're an import / export business. Sounds a bit James Bond, I know, but that's essentially it. We move goods in and out of the UK and all across Europe. That's why we're so close to the port. We have lorries moving through there all day, every day."

"How many people work for you?"

"They work for the company, DI Gray." Langham smiled, sipped his coffee. "There's ninety-two of us. Personally, I'm not involved in the day-to-day activity anymore. I'm here more to provide the overall direction and a mantra to which we operate. I have an executive management team to do all the difficult stuff. Very different to when I first started out with only my truck." Langham nodded towards the largest of the photos on the wall. Langham himself, with a full head of hair, in front of a lorry cab with his name stencilled above the grill. Langham had his arms crossed and chest puffed out. "Things were much simpler back then. God knows what Brexit is going to mean."

Inside, Gray groaned. The last thing he wanted was another bloody political debate. Dover was on the front line of Brexit, France visible across the narrow strip of the English Channel.

Gray wasn't interested. "Jasper Myerscough works for you, sir?"

"That's right. Hard-working and studious, that's why we like him. One of our best people. He's a senior member of our executive team."

"How long has Mr Myerscough been employed by you?"

"Coming up for two years, and not a day goes by when I don't thank the Lord for his details passing over my desk. Jasper manages all the freight movements in and out of the UK. He liaises with the port authority and sometimes Border Forces to ensure the smooth running of our transit. Jasper is absolutely key. We pride ourselves on being above board here. Have to be, otherwise we'd lose a swathe of contracts. It's hard enough to get by already, with the fuel duty and immigration issues. One day Jasper might be dealing with a group of foreigners who've hidden away on our truck, another could be some errant paperwork by one of our customers in Latvia or Romania."

"What about Albania?"

"Of course. We deal with the old Soviet bloc quite a bit. Look, what's this all got to do with Jasper? We're just a big family at Langham's, DI Gray, which is why we've all been so worried, him getting taken sick so suddenly. Is he all right? We haven't heard since he called in."

"When was that?"

"Three days ago." Langham leant forward. "Why are you here, DI Gray?"

"Mr Myerscough has been reported missing by his wife."

"Sweet Jesus." Langham sat back. "Wife, you say?"

"Correct."

"I thought Jasper was single."

"What made you believe so?"

"Jasper regularly put in long hours and I often told him to go home, that nobody when they were on their deathbed wished they'd been at work more. Jasper said he had nothing and no-one to go home to anyway." Gray doubted Sylvia would be happy to hear that nugget of information. "And when we had any gatherings like the Christmas party or a summer barbecue, Jasper came alone."

"Do you spend a lot of time together?" asked Gray.

"What does 'a lot' mean, inspector? Socially, no. I invited him around to my house once for dinner with the family. He came, but it was quite awkward, he barely spoke and seemed like he'd rather be anywhere else so we didn't repeat that error. Here, Jasper keeps himself to himself. We talk about business, of course, what's going on that I need to know about. Sometimes I drop him off at the Kearsney train station, but that's only a few minutes away in the car."

"He doesn't drive here?"

"Jasper's one for public transport. If he needs to get down to the port to see anybody he uses our pool car."

"How often does Mr Myerscough visit the port?"

Langham shrugged. "As much as is needed. It all depends on if there are any problems or not."

"Just take a rough guess, Mr Langham."

"Sometimes every day, others not for a week. It's impossible to be specific, inspector. Why does this matter?"

"At the moment I'm simply asking questions. Who does he go and see?"

"Again, it varies according to the situation. I can get names if you like?"

"That would be much appreciated, thank you."

"Wait here." Langham stood.

"And would you also be able to let me know what address you have on file for Mr Myerscough?"

"No problem. I'll be back shortly." Langham left the room. While he waited, Gray studied the other photos on the wall. There was a group shot of presumably every employee lined up in front on three Langham trucks. The vehicles were arranged like the petals of a flower – one central, two at 45 degrees. The staff stood in rows, like in a school photo, with Langham front and centre. Gray leaned in to get a closer look. At Langham's shoulder stood a grinning Myerscough.

The door opened. Langham, with a piece of paper which he held out. "I'm sorry it took me a little longer than I thought.

The address was easy, but Jasper has several contacts at the port."

"Thank you, Mr Langham." Gray took the document, read the names and Myerscough's address, which was correct. "Do your vehicles ever come through the tunnel?" The route from Folkestone, another quarter of an hour or so along the dual carriageway.

"Everything goes via Dover, it's the lowest cost option for us. Would you let me know when you find him?"

"Of course."

"And what is his wife's name?"

"Sylvia."

"Do you think she'd mind me getting in touch? I'd like to send her my best wishes."

"I'll ask her."

"Thank you, Inspector Gray. This is my business card with all my contact details." Gray accepted the card. "Is that everything?"

"It's all I can think of right now."

"Then let me show you out."

At the exit Langham shook Gray's hand. "I hope the information I've given you proves helpful."

In his car Gray's phone rang. It was Pfeffer. She said, "Sir, we've had a report. A vehicle has been found abandoned. The plate is registered to a Jasper Myerscough. Thought you might like to know."

"Where's the car?" asked Gray.

Thirteen

Gray drove past the Norman church, known locally as the Cathedral on the Marshes, which towered over the village of Minster; a small settlement with a long monastic history, on the southern edge of Thanet. Nearby were the ruins of an abbey, dating back to Saxon times. Only a few miles away Saint Augustine had landed by boat more than a thousand years ago to bring Christianity to the masses. The marshland was to the south of the village, a large area of boggy, poor land which was a haven for wildlife.

Just beyond the church was the road Gray wanted, imaginatively called Station Approach. A few hundred yards further along, where the name changed to Cheesemans Close, stood a patrol car. Gray turned into the tiny car park, only space for ten vehicles, most of which were occupied. Over to the left stood a small, low building, like a Portacabin, painted a dark blue, the windows boarded up. A plain wooden lattice fence ran along the perimeter and then the railway line. A footbridge immediately opposite the car park entrance allowed access to the other platform.

In the far corner was Myerscough's vehicle, a red Audi A4, barricaded in by a huge blue bin on wheels, police tape, a uniform and Pfeffer. Gray pulled up, got out.

"Morning, sir," said Pfeffer.

"Melanie," said Gray. He nodded to the uniform, a female PC who didn't look old enough to be on the job.

"The car was reported last night by parking enforcement," said Pfeffer. "It was about to be towed when we got a hit on the registration."

Several plastic envelopes with white squares of paper inside were affixed to the windscreen. Three of them. One for each day that Myerscough had been missing.

"We sent someone to pick up a spare set of keys from the wife," continued Pfeffer.

"Good thinking. Has anyone searched the interior?"

"Not yet. I was waiting for you."

"Let's take a look then."

Gray and Pfeffer pulled on a pair of nitrile gloves. He opened the driver's door, Pfeffer took the rear. Gray squatted and leaned in. The faint smell of stale food quickly dissipated. Pfeffer showed him the box and wrapper from a takeaway chicken franchise. Gray opened the glove compartment. The car's instruction manual and a mobile charging cable was all he found.

"Nothing of note," said Gray.

"Or here," replied Pfeffer.

Gray stood, closed the door. The boot was empty. A mat lined the base. Gray lifted it, revealing the spare tyre. He caught sight of something tucked just behind the tyre. He leaned in, pulled it out. A small plastic box with the three concentric rings which was the car manufacturer's logo, rectangular, about nine inches across and six inches wide, maybe an inch deep. Originally intended to hold spare bulbs and fuses. German planning and organisation.

He unclipped the two plastic clasps holding the lid down. It didn't contain emergency electrical items anymore, but small wraps of clear plastic, tied so they held a ball of white powder the diameter of a ten pence piece or an American quarter. He tumbled them out onto the palm of his hand. Five in total. No need for him to say what they looked to be. He returned the wraps to the case, handed it to Pfeffer who had an evidence bag open and ready.

"Get those analysed, please." Gray shut the boot. "And have the car towed. I want Forensics to pull the car apart, see what they can find." He glanced around. "Are there any CCTV cameras?"

"I already checked, sir. Two on the platform, another on the High Street. There may be some private monitoring too, but we'll need to check."

"Show me the station cameras, please."

A yellow line was painted down the middle of the platform, running its length. Both ends were fenced off, blocking access to the track. A bin, overflowing with rubbish, stood against the Portacabin, and an overhead digital sign stated when the next train was due to stop – in thirty-seven minutes. This was the side for heading south, towards Dover.

"There." Pfeffer pointed. Both cameras were mounted on the Portacabin which looked to be an office building for the rail employees. "They seem to be set to give a full view of the platform in both directions."

"Appears so." Gray tried the door, locked. He looked through the windows but it was dark inside.

"Get access to the recording equipment," said Gray. "Soon as you can."

"I'm on it," said Pfeffer. "I'll also start door to door, see if we can track down any sightings of Mr Myerscough." She paused while a train shot past. A high speed service not pausing at Minster. The wash exerted a strong pull on Gray, even though he was right back on the platform.

"Why here?" asked Pfeffer once the train was fading into the distance, taking the racket with it.

"Direct line east into Canterbury," said Gray. "Fifteen minutes, probably. From there straight to London, four trains an hour. Or south, if he wanted down to Dover and over into Europe. And he's got a three-day head start."

"He could be anywhere, then."

"Very true."

"Still think it's a man walking out on his wife?"

"I don't know," said Gray. "But his wife might."

Fourteen

The rain began as Gray turned off Canterbury Road and into Birchington, the car buffeted by a blustery squall which rose suddenly and without warning as they often did on this exposed tip of the county.

Just over ten minutes later, and with his wipers on their highest speed, Gray pulled onto Sylvia's drive, got out and, hunched against the downpour, ran to the front door. He knocked, fast and urgent.

She opened up, recognised Gray and pulled the door wide. "Get yourself inside." He needed no further invite, dripping already from the short exposure. "I'll take your coat," she said once the weather was blocked out.

Gray shrugged off his jacket and handed it to Sylvia. "Thanks."

She hung his coat on the stairs' newel post then pointed along the corridor. "Go through." He headed into the front room which was in exactly the same pristine state as when he'd been here the other day. "One of your officers visited earlier, after Jas's spare keys. Did you find anything?"

"His car abandoned in Minster," said Gray, remaining standing.

"That's all?"

"I was at your husband's employer, Langham's, earlier."

"Finally! And?"

"He seems to have been a model member of staff and they're worried about his welfare. The business owner, Langham himself, wants to reach out to you."

"That's very good of him, Sol. But I'm not keen to speak with anyone right now."

"Have you met Mr Langham?"

Sylvia paused. "No."

"Why?"

"There's never really been the occasion. Jas told me they're not a very social company."

"It's strange, Sylvia, because Langham didn't even know you existed."

"Jas is a very private man."

Which was a strange way to respond.

"And there *have* been social events," said Gray. "Your husband went to Mr Langham's house for dinner once. He told Mr Langham that he had nobody to go home to. That's more than private, Sylvia, it's a lie. Now, why would he say that?"

Sylvia flopped into a chair, put a hand over her face. "Please, sit down will you, Sol? I can't abide you looming over me." Gray took the chair opposite. She continued, "I wasn't entirely honest with you, but hopefully once I explain you'll understand." She folded her hands in her lap.

She continued, "My husband is a free spirit, impossible to tie down. It was great fun at first, particularly as I'd been alone for so long and stuck in a routine. Everything in its place and a place for everything." She smiled weakly. "Then it got frustrating, him railing against me trying to tie him down and control him, wondering where he was when he was out and about, doing whatever. But I loved him and I kept telling myself all was going to be okay.

"Then Jasper asked me to marry him. I was elated. I thought that once we were officially a couple he'd settle down properly and listen to me more. For a while it seemed to work, but when he went missing I knew I'd just been fooling myself."

"Does he ever use drugs?"

"Why?"

"We found some in his car."

Sylvia lowered her eyes. "I thought he'd stopped." She stared at Gray again. "I know what happened between you and Jeff, Solomon. He confided in me every now and again."

Gray paused. "What do you mean, Sylvia?" His stomach churned and his heart began to race. He was sure his face was beginning to turn red too. If Carslake had been open with Sylvia, if she knew the truth...

"Jeff was eaten up about you, what you'd been through, but he said you never stopped battling for the facts. Whatever the consequences. I had two rocks in my life – my job working for Jeff and Jasper. When Jeff died one was gone forever. I can't lose the other, Solomon. I can't lose him, I don't know how I'd cope." Tears began to roll down her cheeks. "I don't know what to do. I'm scared and I'm alone."

Gray watched her cry. Sobs began to wrack her body. He wasn't sure how to react. Should he say something he didn't mean? Hug her? He still felt an antipathy towards her and he wasn't the most tactile of people. He wasn't built for situations like this. Not any more. Nevertheless, he couldn't stand by and do nothing.

"Why don't you show me his room?" he asked. "Maybe there's something I can learn from there."

"You'll help?"

"I'm here, aren't I?"

Sylvia cuffed away her tears before leading him upstairs. She paused on the landing, sniffed, pointed. "This is his. Mine is opposite. We sleep separately." She cast her eyes down, seemingly embarrassed to admit another falsehood. Previously she'd said Myerscough only stayed in the spare front room when he was home late. Gray let it pass.

She showed Gray a key. "He keeps his room locked at all times. I didn't exaggerate when I said Jas is a private man. There's a lot he hasn't told me about himself. But when you're alone in the house all day then curiosity can take over. It was simple to find a locksmith capable of getting in and cutting me a spare."

Sylvia passed the key to Gray. He slid it into the keyhole, twisted. Inside was a simple space – a bed, built-in wardrobe, some books on a shelf, a bedside cabinet, some drawers. The curtains were wide, allowing light to flood in, the view over the garden to the rear of the house.

The wardrobe was full of clothes. A couple of empty metal hangers, but otherwise the contents were fulsome. Same with the drawers – plenty of pants and socks. But Gray didn't have the experience to know whether this was normal or not.

He turned to Sylvia. She lingered in the entrance, arms crossed, as if she was trespassing and uncomfortable doing so, even though it wouldn't be the first time. "How does this look too you?" he asked.

"Like he left with not much more than the clothes he was standing up in," she said.

Which to Gray probably meant Myerscough didn't plan to disappear for long. Unless he'd been planning to buy new clothes wherever he ended up.

"That's not all," said Sylvia. She stepped over the threshold, crossed to the wardrobe, shucked back the clothes. In the wall there was a small safe inset. "Jas recently told me the number. Just in case, he said." She tapped at the keypad.

"Why would he keep the door locked, but tell you the number?"

"Jas is a man of contradictions," she said, like that explained everything. She swung the safe open, stepped back.

Gray took her place. Using a fingertip, he shifted around the items inside.

"Is this enough to intrigue you now, Solomon?" asked Sylvia.

Three passports and a stack of cash, banknotes neatly wrapped in a clear plastic film, sat in the safe.

"And that's what I want, Solomon. For you to dig and keep digging until you hit the bottom."

GRAY ENTERED THE DETECTIVES' Office. Pfeffer was on the phone. She raised a hand in greeting, which Gray returned. In his office he fired up his computer. With Sylvia's permission he had removed the three passports from the safe, but left the cash.

He spread the passports out on his desk. One was burgundy and British. The second appeared very similar, a harp on the front denoting Irish origin. The third was blue and had a large, regal coat of arms on the cover and was issued by Canada. All of them were in the name of Jasper Myerscough.

Gray accessed the Police National Computer database. He tapped in 'Jasper Myerscough'. Zero results were returned – no convictions, warnings, nothing. To all intents, Myerscough was a model, law-abiding citizen. But Gray knew enough now to be sure the man had a deeper history.

Gray remembered Sylvia's words. *Is that enough to intrigue you now, Solomon?*

Yes, it was. But where the hell was Gray going to move from here? Myerscough was a shadow who'd simply disappeared.

Fifteen

Petrela was in her usual space against the fence outside the synagogue. She caught sight of Gray approaching, threw a glance across the road. The same kid Gray had seen yesterday was sitting on a wall, eyes on his phone. She began to fast walk in the opposite direction.

Gray broke into a trot.

Petrela flung a glance over her shoulder, realised Gray was closing, a panicked expression on her face. She ran now, but Gray was too near. Within yards he was on her, grabbing hold of her clothes at the shoulder, dragging her to a halt. She yanked herself free, span, face red, enraged, teeth bared. "What the hell do you want, man?"

Gray showed her his warrant card. "To ask you some questions." Then he unfolded the photo of Jasper Myerscough Sylvia had given him. "Do you know this man?"

Petrela gave the image a brief glance. "Never seen him before." But Gray thought she was lying, sure there had been a flash of recognition in her eyes. "I'm not telling you anything." She looked past Gray, then returned her attention to him. "Disappear, before you regret it."

"Why?" The street was empty, the kid out of sight.

"I suggest you go, before there's trouble. I'd say you've about a minute before he arrives."

"Who?"

Petrela's cheeks turned as pale as milk. All her aggression had gone. She just seemed scared. "You should leave, now." But he didn't. A car, a large dark blue Lexus sedan, glided up beside them. "Whatever happens, it's down to you." She stepped back, adopted a strong pose, grimace on her face, hands clenched. Gray turned.

Kerbside, the passenger window down, engine idling, a man sat in the passenger seat. Shaved head, stubble on his chin, hollow cheeks. "This guy disturbing you, E?" He spoke in an Eastern European accent, showing a broken front tooth when he opened his mouth.

"He's just leaving, aren't you?" said Petrela, eyeing Gray.

"No," said Gray.

The man popped his door, got out. He was tall, a couple inches above Gray. The driver's side opened too. Another guy, black, broader, wearing a leather jacket and jeans, sporting long dreadlocks.

The passenger walked up to Gray, got right into his space. "You after buying something?" Gray could smell tobacco and alcohol.

"He's a cop," said Petrela.

The man shrugged, looked Gray up and down, like he was inspecting rancid meat. From foot to forehead and back again. "He seems like nothing to me," he said and spat on the floor, right beside Gray's shoe, before smiling.

"She's right." Gray pulled out his warrant card, held it out for the passenger.

"I not care about fucking *cops*." The man snatched the card without even glancing at it, tossed it over his shoulder. "We have all cops we need." Gray clenched his fists, ready to fight, if need be.

"Whoa, whoa." The driver got in between the passenger and Gray, facing his friend. Hands up, in a form of surrender. "Let's not do this."

"Get out of my way," said the man, pushing the black guy to one side.

"This isn't how he wants things done, remember, Leka?"

Gray had a name now.

"I'll have to tell him," said the driver. "You know how that'll go."

Who was the driver referring to?

Suddenly, Leka grinned, took a step back, a seemingly different person, clapped the driver on the shoulder. "You are right of course! My apologies, officer." Leka retrieved Gray's warrant card from where it lay. He looked at it properly this time. "Solomon Gray. Detective Inspector." Leka nodded. "Very well done." Leka held out the card. The driver, who'd turned so he was side on to both Gray and Leka, took the card and gave it to Gray. "I see you around, Inspector Gray." Leka walked back to the car and got in.

The driver threw Gray one last glance before he headed to the driver's side. He started the engine and pulled away slowly. All the while Leka was watching Gray in the side mirror.

When they were gone Gray realised that Petrela had made her escape also. She must have slipped away while Gray's attention was on the confrontation. He leant against the wall, allowed his heart rate to slow.

Back inside his car Gray wrote down 'Leka' and a quick description in his notebook, then the same for the black guy. He paused, wondered what Leka had meant when he'd said they had all the cops they needed. Were they paying one of his colleagues?

Gray had to know more about what he might be dealing with, and there was one person to ask.

"ARE YOU ALL RIGHT, sir?" asked Pfeffer when Gray walked into the Detectives' Office. "You look wired."

"Traffic was a nightmare," lied Gray. A terrible reason, but all he could think of On the spot.

"I've just made a pot of coffee," she said. "I'll bring you a cup, if you want, sir?"

"That would be great." Gray entered his office, shrugged off his jacket. He sat, started up his computer as Pfeffer came in. She put the mug on the table in front of him. "Thanks and would you mind closing the door on your way out?"

"Sure," said Pfeffer and then she was gone and he was alone.

Gray picked up the cup. His hand trembled. The brief brush with Leka had shaken him. Leka didn't care Gray was police. There was an arrogance about him that Gray hadn't witnessed before. As if he was untouchable.

Gray pulled out his mobile, scrolled down the contacts until he reached the entry – *Yarrow, Adam*. Gray hadn't seen the DCI since he'd upped and left Thanet at the conclusion of Pivot, an operation to tackle County Lines; drug dealing by gangs who were based outside the area, transporting narcotics in for sale to the locals, and shifting the cash from the sale back to their base. Like an import / export business, but an illegal one.

Yarrow answered within a couple of rings. "Sol, you old bastard, how's things?"

"Less of the old, please."

Yarrow laughed down the line. "How's that wonderful boss of yours?"

"Von's fine." Gray just wanted to get to the subject.

"I'm assuming this isn't a courtesy call?"

"You know me too well."

"Is it about Emily?"

"Actually, no."

"Oh, I thought you were going to give me a hard time to ensure she's posted to Thanet."

"Wherever she goes is her choice."

"Okay." Yarrow sounded slightly awkward now. "Fire away, then."

"I'd like to learn how Albanian gangs operate. One has quietly taken over the drugs trade here."

"What are you seeing?"

"Ironically, not much until we started digging. We've experienced a general drop in crime in recent months. Except overdoses, they're well up."

"Okay."

"I had a chat with a user the other day. He said he and his friends are living in fear of the Albanians. I've been trying to find out more about their network but it's extremely difficult. I've attempted to work upwards from the street though I'm not getting far, fast."

"Sounds about right, Sol. I'm assuming a dealer will only sell to people they know?"

"Correct."

"That's typical. It's a cutout structure. The Albanians have a reputation for being tough bastards. They deal with any threat against them via extreme violence. Fear and intimidation is pretty much standard staple for any drug supplier these days, but the Albanians take it to another level.

"And I'm not surprised you haven't made any progress breaking into their structure. Even the people working within the organisation will be under threat. The criminals know there's only two ways to go down – forensics from direct evidence of handling the drugs, or a witness with irrefutable evidence, like from someone in the organisation we've turned and is feeding us information.

"But when the leaders won't even be seen in the same room as the drugs, a witness is the only way, so the defence mechanism is to ensure the dealers fear recrimination more than the prospect of getting time. I'm telling you, Sol, the boys we cleared up during Pivot are nothing compared to this lot."

"So, we made things worse? Is that what you're saying?"

"Sort of. However, if one of the big gangs wants in there's virtually nothing the incumbents can do about it. They either resist and more than likely end up dead, or get absorbed and agree to work in the new team. More often than not it's the latter course people choose, particularly the lower echelons. They're still getting paid the same. Just a different master, is all."

Yarrow sighed down the phone. "The only way you're going to understand more about these guys is with an undercover, an expert at infiltrating gangs. It'll take months for him or her to work their way up, to build trust."

"Nineteen people have already died, Adam, I don't know whether we have months."

"That's just to gain entry, never mind move anywhere near the top."

"Doing nothing isn't an option."

"I'm not suggesting that at all, Sol. I'm in this shit every day."

"Sorry, you're right."

"Don't apologise. Look, why don't I come down and see you? Pivot is being wound up anyway and all that's getting thrown at me is more and more paperwork. I'll bring a colleague with me, Roza Selimi, she really knows her stuff."

"If that's not a problem."

"I wouldn't offer if it was. And besides, it gives me a chance to get to meet Yvonne again. Fringe benefits and all that." Gray could hear the smile in Yarrow's voice.

"You're on. One more question. How often do you see cops being turned by dealers?"

"Like taking bribes for information?"

"Yes."

"More than you'd think. Some of my colleagues believe that with all the cash washing around in the drug industry and cops rubbing up against it all the time corruption is inevitable and allowable, as long as the results come in. It's a better than 50:50 chance somebody inside your station is working with the outside. It could be for money, it could be plain bribery. Best to assume it's happening and go from there."

"That's depressing."

"And a fact of life. You've just got to accept it."

Yarrow's typical straightforward answers had given Gray plenty to think about. "Anyway, when can we expect you?"

"How's tonight sound? We can drive down from Colchester in a couple of hours. I'll book the same hotel as last time, the one by the train station in Margate."

"Look forward to it."

Gray ended the call. Now he just had to let Hamson know they'd be having visitors.

We have all the cops we need.

Pfeffer knocked on Gray's door. "There's a report of a man being found at the base of the Margate cliffs," she said.

"A jumper?" asked Gray.

Pfeffer pulled a face. "He was pushed. Two men in plain sight shoved him over near the Bethesda Medical Centre in Palm Bay." Which wasn't far from Odell House. "Seems like they weren't trying to hide it. Amazingly he survived but he's in a bad way."

"Have we got a name?"

"No, but there's a photo." Pfeffer showed Gray. He recognised the man immediately.

Sixteen

Gray walked through the main entrance of the Queen Elizabeth The Queen Mother hospital on the edge of Margate. He'd visited many times before, most often to see the pathologist, Ben Clough. That didn't mean he knew his way around it, though.

The original Victorian building, which Gray was in, had been modified and added to over the years, creating a warren of corridors, wards and treatment rooms. Gray checked the signs on the wall, headed in the direction the arrow pointed.

The patient lay behind drawn curtains in a general ward with five others. The room smelt – boiled cabbage, presumably from dinner, and body odour despite the open window at the far end.

Both the man's legs were lifted in traction. There was a drip beside his head, a tube running into his left arm. By his other hand sat a controller unit, for raising and lowering the bed, with a wire snaking back to the headboard. He was cased from hip to foot in white plaster, a stark contrast to his black skin. Somebody had written, 'Stay lucky' in blue pen on the nearest thigh.

Gray picked up the chart on the flip-pad hanging off the end of the bed, just to see if the victim had been identified yet – one of his past bosses would certainly have pretended to know what all the jargon meant, whereas Gray was clueless as to that stuff. The space for a name said 'Joseph'.

Joseph's eyes flickered open, tried to focus on Gray, then recognition settled in. It was the driver who'd intervened between Leka and Gray on Godwin Road. His fingers felt for the controller unit. Gray reached it first. He didn't want the man calling a nurse, not before they'd spoken.

"Who did this to you?" asked Gray.

"I don't need no more trouble."

"Was it Leka?" No response. "I can help."

"That's what got me here. I should have just let you take a beating. I won't be pressing charges."

"That's not your choice."

"Piss off." Joseph turned away from Gray, stared at the window.

Gray dropped the controller next to the patient and walked out of the ward.

When he drove out of the car park he passed the smokers standing on the pavement, officially off hospital property. There used to be designated areas, but even these were banned now. One man in a dressing gown beside a drip on a stand with wheels. The pull of nicotine.

As Gray glanced towards the traffic he caught sight of a face he recognised. Leka. He was leaning against the wall, a cigarette dangling from his grinning lips. Gray bumped his car onto the pavement, set the hazard lights flicking and made his way over.

"Inspector Gray," said Leka, then blew out a long stream of white smoke right at him.

"What're you doing here?" asked Gray.

"Free country. Or has UK turned into police state?"

"I asked you a question."

Leka took another draw on his half-finished tab. "Visiting a friend."

"Was it you that signed his cast?"

"Who?"

"Joseph."

"My mother is sick."

"What's her name? I'll pay her a visit and give her my best," said Gray.

Leka took another drag, dropped the stub on the tarmac, didn't bother to grind it out. "Stay lucky, inspector." Leka turned and walked away.

GRAY DROVE UP FORT Hill but carried on past Odell House and towards Cliftonville. He slowed near the Bethesda Centre, a walk-in NHS clinic used by the local drug addicts trying to quit – here they got their weekly allocation of methadone.

The turning he wanted was just after the tennis courts, a narrow incline called Sackett's Gap, which dropped down to the esplanade. Gray parked at the base of the cliff next to a cafe.

A hundred yards or so away the promenade ended, or started, depending upon your perspective. The promenade ran all the way to the harbour arm on the main Margate sands. A set of steps gave access onto the beach, which was mainly sand dotted with rock pools. The tide was high and receding. Gray paused roughly where Joseph had been thrown off the cliff. The sand was unblemished, washed clean by the waters.

Gray assumed the perpetrators had deliberately chosen this spot, the soft sand. Injury was more likely than death. Dampness was seeping into Gray's shoes. He turned around and walked back. Nothing to see here. As he reached his car his phone rang.

"Have you spoken with Worthington yet?" asked Hamson.

"I haven't had a chance."

"Christ's sake, Sol. I've had another complaint."

"Who against?"

"Worthington, of course."

"I'll deal with him as soon as I get in," promised Gray. He could do with someone to take his frustration out on.

Seventeen

Gray walked straight over to Worthington's desk. The DC was tapping away at his keyboard.

"Jerry, I'd like a word," said Gray. "Several words, actually."

Worthington didn't even glance up, carried on with his work. "Can it wait, sir? I'm just in the middle of something."

"No." Gray spoke through gritted teeth, all he could do to hold back the anger. He couldn't lose his temper, not here in the office.

Now Worthington looked at Gray. There was a hint of amusement on his lips. "What's getting your goat now, boss?"

"We'll discuss that in my office." Gray turned away, headed to his office.

Gray hung his jacket on a hook, stood for a few moments expecting Worthington to arrive straight away. But Worthington remained at his desk, tapping away at the keyboard. Gray leant against the door jamb, arms crossed, foot tapping. Still Worthington didn't look up.

"DC Worthington," said Gray. "I'm waiting."

Worthington held up a hand. "One sec, sir."

"Jesus," said Gray.

Still focused on his screen Worthington slowly rose. He tapped away at the keys a couple more times before finally turning to Gray. "I'm getting a brew, sir. Want one?"

"Get here, now."

"What's got into you?"

"Close the door," said Gray when Worthington was inside. "Sit down."

Worthington took the chair in front of the desk. "Sir?"

Gray remained standing. "I've received some rather concerning feedback regarding your actions recently."

Worthington frowned. "Such as?"

"That you've made racially tinged statements towards one of your colleagues."

Worthington's cheeks reddened. "What am I supposed to have said? And to who?"

"Take a wild guess."

Worthington shrugged. "As I haven't said anything, I wouldn't know."

"DC Pfeffer."

"That's a surprise, sir." Worthington blinked. "I've been perfectly polite to Mel showing her the ropes and everything."

"That's not what I understand."

"Is it her that's complained?"

"Actually, no. It's not."

"Then who?"

"I've witnessed how you behaved with DC Pfeffer myself. Down on the Ramsgate promenade."

Worthington's brow creased while he searched his memory. "I can't remember saying anything 'racially tinged'."

"You asked her to buy a bacon sandwich."

Worthington made to look surprised. "Hadaway, sir. Is that a crime? If so, I'll turn myself in now. Along with most of Thanet. Bacon is pretty popular."

"You know she's Jewish."

"Sorry, sir, I don't understand."

"I saw the expression on your face when Doctor Clough mentioned her heritage."

Worthington threw his hands up in the air. "This is all bullshit. Somebody has got it in for me, because they're worried."

"Worried?"

"Competition for the sergeant's role, maybe?"

"It's not vacant."

"Not yet, but it will be when Ibbottson finally does the decent thing and retires on medical grounds."

"You think you're a shoo-in for the role, constable?"

"Nobody else is capable. I'm the best person for the job. Surely you can see that."

"What's your problem with DC Pfeffer?"

Worthington leaned forward. "I don't have anything against DC Pfeffer. It's not her fault she's a kike."

Gray didn't respond, watched Worthington's features shift as he realised what he'd said. "I don't want to hear nor witness further derogatory statements towards DC Pfeffer, or anyone else for that matter. If the slightest mention comes to my attention then we will be talking again and on a formal basis with HR included. Do I make myself clear?"

"This is favouritism."

"What are you on about?"

"You prefer her to me, to everyone else. She gets away with stuff I never would. She's always in and out of your office, bringing you drinks" Worthington stood. "I'm going to make a complaint to DCI Hamson about you and her. Something's going on. Maybe you're shagging her."

"Feel free to speak with DCI Hamson, I've nothing to hide."

"I will." Worthington nodded to himself.

"In the meantime are we clear on my expectations as to your behaviour towards DC Pfeffer?"

"Crystal, sir." Worthington's tone was sharp and he fixed Gray with a hard stare. He wasn't backing down at all.

"You're dismissed."

The DC departed without another word, slamming the door shut behind him. Gray picked up his phone, tapped out Hamson's internal number.

"I've just spoken to Worthington about Pfeffer. It didn't go so well. He maintained his innocence and then dropped out a racist word – kike."

"Jesus."

"Then he accused me of favouring Pfeffer and having an affair with her. He may come up and speak with you to lodge an official complaint."

"Fighting fire with fire."

"So it seems."

"All right, let's play this by the book. Write an email to me outlining the conversation you've just had with Worthington. Then we've got a record. Likewise with any future discussions."

"What about DC Pfeffer?"

"You've had a word with her already, right?"

"Yes."

"Then leave her. If Worthington sees you approach her now it'll just add fuel to the fire. And now somebody's knocking at my door."

"Probably Worthington."

"I'll catch you later." Hamson ended the call.

Gray's mobile rang. Yarrow. Gray rejected the call, wanting to focus on the email to Hamson while the conversation with Worthington was still fresh in his mind. Nearly a quarter of an hour later, he sent the email and rang Yarrow back.

"Sorry about that. I was in the middle of something."

"No problem. It's just to let you know, I couldn't get that hotel by the train station. Anywhere else you can suggest?"

"Try The Albion in Broadstairs. It's near my flat, and there's plenty of restaurants just down the road."

"Great, I'll do that. I'll call when we're in and settled. By the way, is Yvonne coming along?"

"I haven't asked."

"We can only stay the night, I don't have the time to come into the office tomorrow so I figured we could all talk together, then Roza and I will head back in the morning."

"In that case I'll book us a table at a restaurant and ensure Yvonne is there."

"Good man. See you later."

Gray disconnected. He hoped Yarrow and his colleague would be able to give him some answers.

Eighteen

The Albion was a grand old pile on Albion Street, above the main Viking Bay and popular with the tourists. Charles Dickens had written one of his books here while holidaying. Or at least a blue plaque on the outside of the building said so.

Yarrow was waiting for Gray in the hotel lobby, leaning on the reception desk and chatting to the young woman seated behind. He was a tall man with a shock of white hair, a large nose and a pockmarked face; acne scars from youth in all likelihood. Yarrow's older appearance clashed with the colourful friendship bands he wore on his left wrist, the ends frayed.

Beside Yarrow was a short woman with jet black hair which reached down to her waist. When Yarrow caught sight of Gray he broke off from the conversation with the receptionist and walked over to Gray, a smile splitting his face. He shook Gray's hand before turning to his colleague. "Sol, this is Roza Selimi."

"Pleased to meet you," she said, smiling too, though with more reserve than Yarrow. Her accent was similar to Leka's. Brown eyes set into a round face, olive skin, a scar beneath her lip she hadn't bothered to bury under make-up.

"I've booked us a table at a restaurant down the hill," said Gray.

"Where's DCI Hamson?" asked Yarrow.

"She's meeting us there."

"Come on then, what are we waiting for?"

Albion Street was a narrow thoroughfare which ran parallel with the cliff, packed with restaurants, cafes and pubs. The pavement was only wide enough for one person so Yarrow and Roza followed Gray in single file. He led them past the small and formal Balmoral Gardens which nestled between the high buildings either side.

A few hundred yards along Gray turned onto Harbour Street. The road dropped towards the beach and the jetty. Viking Bay was framed through an arch, what used to be a portcullis when the fishing village was threatened by Scandinavian seaborne raiders hundreds of years ago.

Gray paused outside the restaurant. "This is it," he said, and entered.

Hamson was already at the bar, holding a glass of white wine. Yarrow crossed to her, took her free hand, raised it to his lips and planted a kiss.

A waitress came from behind the bar. "Good evening," she said. "A table for four?"

"I have one booked already, name of Gray."

"If you'll follow me."

The layout was a series of floors, like large steps, which tracked the contours of the hill. They were shepherded to the lowest level and given a round table barely large enough for them, opposite the open galley kitchen. The chairs were mismatched and the table wobbled slightly, but that was an intended charm, Gray knew. A large plate-glass window delivered a view of Harbour Street and the lights of Broadstairs, up on the cliff.

"Very nice," said Yarrow when they were seated, ordered drinks, taken menus and been told what the specials were. Yarrow had ensured he was next to Hamson, with Gray opposite and Roza in the remaining space.

"Used to be owned by Frank McGavin, the guy who ran Thanet before the Albanians arrived," said Gray. McGavin was abroad, in Northern Cyprus to be exact, avoiding extradition. The new owners continued to specialise in locally sourced ingredients.

"So," said Gray, "you said Pivot is coming to an end."

"As all good things must," said Yarrow, glancing over the menu. "It's been a great run, though."

"What's next?"

"I'm not entirely sure."

"The National Crime Agency?" asked Hamson. The NCA was a UK-wide police force with the objective to target serious organised crime – child exploitation, trafficking and slavery, cyber crime, money laundering and illegal firearms. Emily Wyatt, Gray's partner, had been part of the NCA before joining Yarrow's Pivot team.

Yarrow pulled a face. "Probably not, Yvonne. I don't like how they operate. I think we need to behave in a much more coordinated fashion across the forces. The NCA doesn't have enough autonomy."

"That won't be easy," said Hamson.

"Politics is a massive issue, I agree. But look at the Kent and Essex Serious Crime Directive. That's worked really well." Yarrow pointed his menu at Hamson. Two senior cops chewing over their issues. "Illicit national and transnational criminal networks generate £1.5T revenue globally, £37B in the UK alone. That's nearly two per cent of GDP for God's sake! Well over 4,000 gangs, more than 30,000 people working in them, and a couple of thousand county lines. In 2017 alone, drugs killed 2,500 people. Why isn't that all over the news?

"It's like a bloody industry on its own. And we're expected to keep acting the way we did a hundred years ago? Crazy." Yarrow put down his menu, shook his head. He picked up a piece of bread from a basket in the centre of the table, began to butter it. "We're local and fragmented. I want to change that. You know, when I think back to the 90s it was pretty straightforward. None of this computer stuff going on. Then bank robbers were the top dogs, they earned the most money, but along came the first generation of drug dealers and changed everything. Now narcotics was how you made serious cash.

"The second generation of dealers got themselves educated, read around the subject, how others worked, how the police worked. They ran their businesses like any other legitimate, high value company. They became vertically integrated, controlling the supply chain from top to bottom; buying the gear in South America to running the street. The ecstasy culture shifted behaviours again. All that love in one place. The gangsters saw an opportunity to work together, rather than be in opposition. They realised they were stronger in partnership. They were better integrated then than we are even now!

"Violence was controlled and applied only when needed. There was a code. However," Yarrow shook his head. "With the current generation three we've the Playstation gangsters. They've killed off the previous honour system. The viciousness has skyrocketed. And we're locked into an arms race, neither side can blink, which just exacerbates the culture of fear and intimidation. There has to be a better way."

"That's quite a speech," said Hamson.

"Sorry, it's a passion. Cost me my marriage if I'm honest. I'm hoping the bosses will listen and put me in the right place."

Their waitress, a short young woman with silver hair out of a bottle, came to the table and asked, "Are you ready to order?"

They were and did – starters (except Roza) and main courses.

"What's going on then, Sol?" asked Yarrow. "When we spoke you mentioned Albanians."

"It seems there's a new gang in Thanet. I've met one of them, called Leka. Nasty piece of work. I'd like to understand what I'm dealing with."

"The Albanians are common in the drug trade. Initially we came across them more for people trafficking and the sex trade, but their foray into drugs has boomed. They're now one of the biggest narcotics manufacturer's globally. Another massive company like structure, employing thousands.

"Three years ago the Albanians were the sixth largest UK group recorded in the NCA's organised criminal group mapping project, fifth if you exclude the British gangsters. By the end of 2017 they overtook the Romanians, making them the second biggest foreign criminal gang. So Albanians are a hot topic," said Yarrow. "Roza here is our resident expert in Pivot." Yarrow offered the bread basket around the table, Hamson took a slice. "Why don't you tell us a bit more, Roza?"

"Have you heard of the Silk Road, Inspector Gray?" asked Roza.

"Sol is fine and that's an ancient trade route, right? I remember seeing something on TV."

"Correct, however there's much more than just one course. The Silk Road is an entire network criss-crossing countries and regions, dating back over two hundred years before Christ. Originally the road ran East – West across China transporting silk but over time the system extended to connect Asia with Africa and Europe.

"One of these extensions was a maritime passage, beginning in Lekaandria, crossing the Red Sea then the Indian Ocean to the ports of the western coast of India. From there traders headed to Bactria; now Afghanistan, Tajikistan, and Uzbekistan, navigated the Caspian Sea before reaching the territories of Albania, Iberia and Georgia, Colchis as it used to be called, reaching all the way to Rome."

"Nice history lesson," said Hamson. "But what's the relevance?"

"The Silk Road was also a means of transmitting culture and communications great distances, for one region to influence another, using the movement of goods as the basis for doing so. Partially, that's what's happening in your country now. However, the goods this time are drugs. All my countrymen are doing are utilising pre-existing routes to do so."

The waitress arrived with the starters, interrupting Roza. Yarrow dug into his, a pate with thin slices of lightly browned toast. Gray had ordered the same.

Roza continued, "I was born in Durres, Albania's second city. My older brother, he was an undercover policeman posing as a gang member. Until the gang found out and killed him as an example to others."

"I'm sorry," said Hamson.

"I moved to England to get away, but I haven't really." Roza drank some water. "Albanian gangs are known as the Mafia Shqiptare, there are probably fifteen to twenty in my home country alone. Bribery and corruption is rife. They are very hard to infiltrate and the people involved are largely untouchable. The structure is deeply reliant on loyalty, honour, and family through blood relations and connections by marriage."

Gray stopped eating and listened intently.

Roza continued, "The typical structure of the Albanian mafia is a hierarchy, like the Russians. A family clan is called a *fis* or a *fare*. Clans contain a leadership group known as a *Bajrak*. They behave like a committee. First they select a high-ranking member to run each unit. The unit is led by a *Krye*, which means the boss, who then selects *Kryetar* to serve under them. The *Kryetar* will then choose a *Mik* as a right hand man who liaises with the gang members and is responsible for coordinating all the unit activities and reporting back to the people above."

Their waitress arrived back at the table. "Are you finished?" she asked.

"We are," said Gray.

"That was really good," said Yarrow.

The waitress smiled and she cleared the plates away. Gray was impatient to hear more. "Go on, Roza."

"So, I said they are like a family but one that rules by fear rather than love. *Besaas* is their word for code of honour. We have a saying in our country. *Më mirë syri sesa nami.* It means, better lose your eye than your honour.

"There is a strong discipline with clear rules. Anyone who breaks these rules is dealt with. If you betray the family the price is steep. Punishment brings fear, and fear guarantees total loyalty to the family."

"Is that what happened to your brother?" asked Hamson.

"He was too rash. When faced with a dangerous animal it is best to tread lightly, carefully and slowly. My brother did none of those things and it cost him his life. It is how things are in my country." Roza shrugged. "I only tell you so you are aware what kind of people you are dealing with."

A silence fell across the table. The main course arrived. Hamson and Roza got theirs first, with Yarrow and Gray following shortly after and they ate quietly for a while.

"One aspect we've noticed," said Gray eventually when he felt enough time had passed, "is mainly the same dealers are in place as before. Does that sound typical?"

"Members of other ethnic groups are used, but only for basic tasks and sometimes just the once. English people would be considered like this."

Ironic, thought Gray, *that locals would be considered the foreigners.*

"The close-knit nature of the gangs insulates them from outsiders and thwarts police efforts to infiltrate their networks. The further you go up the tree the more you'll find the power and all of them will be Albanian. But as I said, that is very hard."

"So you don't think I'd be able to break into their gang?" asked Gray.

"I would say no," said Roza.

"Then what do you suggest?"

"Hope for some luck. I am sorry I cannot be more helpful."

"One dealer I've been speaking with is Albanian."

"Oh," said Roza. "That is unusual."

"Why?"

"Perhaps they owe something to somebody and are working off a debt? It is difficult to know. There is not much more I can tell you."

"You've been great, Roza, thanks," said Gray.

"Anyway," said Yarrow, "enough work talk for the moment."

"You're right," said Hamson.

They ate in silence until Yarrow pushed his plate to one side, said, "Anyone for dessert?"

"I couldn't eat another thing," replied Hamson. Gray raised his hands in surrender too.

"I'll pay for dinner."

"Not a chance. You're our guests, it's on me." Hamson raised a hand, got the waitress' attention, made the universal hand signal for the bill.

"Thank you," said Yarrow. "In that case, let me buy you a drink."

"Okay." Hamson nodded.

"I will pass," said Roza. "I am rather tired."

The waitress brought the bill and a card machine. Hamson settled up and they left the restaurant. At the top of Harbour Street Yarrow paused. There were three pubs, one on each corner of the intersection with another across the road. Two were rowdy, targeting the younger generation, the other quiet and more family orientated.

"Which do you suggest?" asked Yarrow.

"There's a better place down here," said Gray. A few yards nearer the hotel along Albion Street Gray paused outside a craft beer bar which had once been a second hand book shop. You could still buy books, but sales were mostly alcohol related now. And a few pies.

"Are you joining us, Sol?" asked Hamson.

"I'll walk Roza back to the hotel," said Gray receiving a glare from Hamson when she realised it was just her and Yarrow. He, on the other hand, appeared delighted. Gray shook Yarrow's hand. "Thanks for coming down."

"My pleasure. Call me if you need anything else." Yarrow headed inside the bar, followed by Hamson.

Outside the hotel Gray stopped again. "This is you."

Roza held out a card. "Here is my number. If you want to know something please just call."

"Thank you."

Roza grabbed Gray on the forearm. "Be very careful," she said. "These are extremely dangerous men. I promise you've never come across anyone like them before. As I said earlier you will need to proceed with care and caution."

"I will."

Roza let go, nodded and went into the hotel. Gray walked back to his flat along the cliff top, the beat of the waves on the shore beneath him, all the while thinking through what Roza had said in the restaurant. Although he'd learnt a lot about the Albanians, he hadn't been given a method to handle them.

Gray's default approach was to shake things up, see what fell out. But Roza had counselled against doing so. Trouble was, Gray didn't know what else to do…

Nineteen

The following morning Gray was at his desk when Hamson entered.

"How was your drink with Yarrow?" asked Gray. He couldn't help but smile.

"It's not funny," said Hamson. "And don't ever do that to me again."

"He's a good guy."

"Maybe, but he's recently divorced, did you know?"

"So what? Anyway, I thought you wanted a relationship."

"Not with a bloody copper!"

"Beggars can't be choosers."

"Oh, that's lovely. Thanks."

"You're welcome."

There was a knock, Pfeffer standing in the doorway to his office. "Sorry, ma'am." She focused on Gray. "Sir, I've got something," said Pfeffer, her words a rush. "Well, two things actually."

"What, Melanie?"

"It's best I show you. Can I use your computer?"

Gray pushed back from his desk, stood. "All yours."

Pfeffer moved Gray's chair into the corner, bent over and rattled at the keyboard. Hamson raised an eyebrow at Gray. "The train operator finally came back with the CCTV from the Minster station," said Pfeffer.

"About bloody time."

"There's been a strike."

"Again? It's like being back in the '70s."

"I wouldn't know, sir." Gray glanced at Pfeffer to see if she was trying to be funny, but the DC was concentrating on her task, biting her bottom lip. Hamson smirked. "I went over the footage from the day Myerscough disappeared," said Pfeffer. "I found this." Pfeffer pointed at the screen.

Where Gray had expected to see a concrete platform and metal rails through the lens, there were clouds scudding across a dark sky and the swaying leaves of some treetops. "The other view is the same." Pfeffer clicked. The perspective was slightly different due to the placement of the second camera, but neither showed what they should. The time on the counter in the corner of the screen was 08.03.

"No bloody use then," said Gray.

"Hang on." Pfeffer clicked at the keys again. "This is from the day before."

The perspective now was as Gray had initially expected. A handful of people standing on the platform, most concentrating on their phones. A train arrived, moving across the screen from right to left. The people dragged their attention away from the mobile devices, got onto the train. Pfeffer paused the footage. She tapped Gray's monitor. "That's Myerscough."

Gray leaned in, Hamson at his shoulder. The image was slightly blurry, the man glancing over his shoulder. "Are you sure?"

"Sure enough. I've gone back through the previous days. It's him. Same time, same place."

"This is the day before he went missing, you say?" asked Gray.

"Right." Pfeffer poked at the keys again. There was a change, now the footage showed brightness in the foreground, the spilling of light from an overhead illumination, darkness in the distance. The clock in the corner now read 01.07. Then the aspect jerked upwards and the camera was staring at sky. Pfeffer paused the playback. "The same happens to the other camera."

"So at night when there aren't any trains due and sensible people are in bed the cameras get moved."

"Yes, sir."

"And then Myerscough disappears," said Gray.

"Seemingly, yes."

"He didn't want us to see which train he got onto."

"That's not it at all." Pfeffer pulled up yet another piece of footage. The view was a fisheye lens looking onto a neat garden, a wooden picket fence just beyond, a house across the road. Someone's arm was on the right of the screen, up close. They walked away, a woman with a dog. She went through the gate, turned right away from the camera. A few seconds later somebody passed by in the opposite direction. The playback cut off.

"Door-to-door found this. A retired woman has one of those doorbell cameras. They activate when there's movement and record for at least thirty seconds." She clicked again. Now there was a still shot on Gray's monitor, a close up of the passerby. "It's HD quality."

"Myerscough," said Gray. And he was carrying a backpack over one shoulder.

"Yes, sir. Just after 7am."

"Where is this?"

"Marsh Farm Road, along from the station." Pfeffer opened up an internet browser, entered a common map webpage, tapped in the address. At the top of the screen was the station. Marsh Farm Road was a long strip leading south and away from Minster. "He'd have crossed the tracks to get there. I rang the dog walker. She said she has a camera because there's been a bit of trouble in the village, particularly on the outskirts. We were very lucky. If Myerscough had passed a few seconds sooner or later we'd have missed him."

"What's down there? At the end of the road."

"Apparently nothing, sir. Just a footpath into the marshland."

And Myerscough was carrying a backpack. Maybe he hadn't gone far at all.

Twenty

Gray's mobile rang then. "Sorry," he said to Pfeffer before answering, "DI Gray." Pfeffer and Hamson started to leave his office.

"Morning, Inspector. My name is Angus Lowther, I'm with the NCA."

Gray stood, motioned for Hamson to come back.

"Morning, Mr Lowther." Gray noticed Lowther didn't supply his rank.

When Hamson was in Gray's office once more he shut his door. She mouthed, "What?"

"Angus is fine, Solomon," said Lowther.

"I prefer Sol," said Gray. "And what can I do for the NCA?"

Hamson raised a surprised eyebrow. Gray put the mobile on speaker so Hamson could hear.

"I'm calling about Jasper Myerscough," said Lowther. "I understand you've been working his case."

"Working is hardly what I'd call it. What's your interest, specifically?"

"I'm afraid I can't go into details."

"Why?"

"It's related to a specific and highly sensitive case. The best I can say is Mr Myerscough has been helping us and he has some key information I need to get from him."

"So, you don't know where he is either?"

"Clearly not." Lowther was starting to sound exasperated. "I thought a courtesy call to you was the right place to start."

"With all due respect, I don't know you."

"In the interests of national safety I simply can't go into details over the phone. Mr Myerscough is important to me and to others. We want to find him. And quickly."

"Who's we?"

"I can't go into that, either."

"Then I don't see how I can help you."

"Perhaps I should ring DCI Hamson, or maybe Superintendent Marsh instead?"

Gray was interested that Lowther had raised the stakes so quickly. "Feel free to do as you wish, Mr Lowther."

Lowther sighed down the line, a heavy exhale. "Look, Sol. I apologise, it's been a difficult couple of weeks and I'm taking it out on you. All I'm asking for is some cooperation between fellow officers. Would you mind keeping me informed of your progress?"

"Do you have an email address I can contact you on?" asked Gray.

"Best if you ring me on this number. It'll be in your call log, right?"

"I'll do what I can."

"That's all I ask. Thank you." Lowther disconnected.

"What the hell was that all about?" asked Hamson.

"I wish I knew. But someone might."

Gray accessed his contact list, saved Lowther's number for future reference. Then he placed a call, kept the phone on speaker.

"Emily, hi, it's Sol," said Gray.

"Yes, I know, your number came up on my screen."

"Have you heard of somebody called Angus Lowther?"

"No 'how are you doing, Emily?' Or, 'I miss you', perhaps? I'm fine, thanks for not asking."

"Sorry, I've just had a strange call and it's bugging me."

"From this Lowther you're asking about?"

"That's right. He said he's NCA. I thought you might be able to help."

"I've never heard of him."

"Oh."

"But I can ask a few old friends if that would help?"

"Yes, please. But be discreet."

"I'm capable of subterfuge, remember?" Gray and Wyatt had kept their relationship under wraps since the beginning. "I'm hoping to come down at the weekend. Are you around?"

"I'm sure I can be."

"Good, we need to spend some time together. And maybe I'll have something for you."

"About Lowther?"

"Maybe something else."

"Ah," the innuendo penny dropped. Gray felt himself flush. Hamson covered up a snigger. "That's more than fine by me."

"I've got to go, Sol. Speak to you later." Wyatt rang off.

"Very strange," said Hamson.

"I agree."

"Keep me up to date on whatever Emily comes back with. I don't like the NCA sniffing around."

"Me either."

"Who's Myerscough running from? The NCA, someone else, or both of them?"

Gray didn't have a clue.

Twenty One

"Anyone seen Melanie?" asked Gray when he entered the Detectives' Office.

A couple of officers shook their heads. Worthington didn't bother responding at all. Gray pulled out his mobile, called Pfeffer. She answered on the second ring.

"Where are you?" he asked.

"In the ladies, if you must know."

"Ah, sorry."

"What's so urgent?"

"I need your help."

"With what?"

"Do you have access to the synagogue on Albion Road?"

"Sir?"

"Like, are you able to get in when there's not a service?"

"I haven't had reason to try."

"Can you?"

"When?"

"Now?"

"Sir, I'm confused."

"Just try and I'll explain later."

"Okay, I'll make a call."

"Come and find me when you're done."

Pfeffer arrived in Gray's office a few minutes' later. "I spoke to the rabbi," she said. "He'll meet us there in fifteen minutes."

"Great, get your coat and bring your phone."

With a frown Pfeffer asked "What's going on?"

"I want you to take a photo of someone for me."

GRAY PARKED ON STANLEY Road, a couple of streets away from Godwin Road. "Sir, are you going to tell me now?"

He turned off the engine. They had a little time before the rabbi was due to arrive, and Pfeffer needed to be briefed. She was holding a camera on her lap. "I've been trying to understand what happened to Nolan and the other overdoses. I haven't learned much so far. All I'm aware of is there's an Albanian gang supplying drugs into Thanet. They took over from the previous supplier, Frank McGavin."

"Okay."

"There's a dealer who works just outside the synagogue."

Pfeffer's face darkened. "I've seen her. Lots of tattoos?"

"That's right, she's called Petrela."

"I know. I've had words, but she ignored me. And it's a shul, not a synagogue."

"A couple of days ago I tried to tap her for information," said Gray, "however somebody called Leka and his driver turned up. It got a bit fruity until the driver intervened and they cleared off. It was the driver who ended up in hospital yesterday, guy called Joseph. He's refusing to press charges or discuss what happened, so that's a dead end. I'm hoping Leka will charge over again when I start talking to Petrela. I want you to take photos of anyone in the immediate vicinity. Maybe we can get some further identification and start to dig in."

"I'll do my best." Pfeffer checked the clock on the dashboard. "He should be here by now."

The rabbi, a short, balding man with wispy grey hair and wearing a skull cap, was waiting for them inside the porch entrance to the building, around the corner from Petrela and concealed from her.

"Sir, this is Amit Rothschild," said Pfeffer.

Rothschild and Gray shook hands. "Let's go inside," said Rothschild. They entered. Rothschild closed the heavy wooden door behind them, the sound echoing through the interior. Where the exterior was austere – boring brown brick and barred windows, inside was height, light and warmth. "Welcome to our humble place of worship," said Rothschild.

There were two floors. Here on the ground there were lines of dark wooden seats, facing forward. At the far end was a large domed window, made up of smaller, individual panes, set into the apex of the wall above a dais. The dome allowed a flood of light to enter. Beneath the dome was what seemed to be an elaborately decorated cabinet and to the right of that a dais. The walls were painted white, the floor a pale wood, planks laid out in the same direction as the seats. Columns and pillars appeared to hold up the carved ceiling, giving the impression of grandeur and height.

However, Gray quickly saw the flaws. There were dust motes in the air, and a thick layer of dirt over the windows. Some water stains created brown patches where ceiling met wall, likely because the roof was leaking. And against the far wall, just to the right of the dome, was some scaffolding. This was a building well past its best and struggling to stay whole. Gray remembered Pfeffer saying there weren't many Jews in

Thanet and those that were here were leaving. Few worshippers meant little money flowing in.

"Are you familiar with shuls?" asked Rothschild.

"This is my first time inside one," said Gray. "And why call it a shul I stead of a synagogue?"

"Because we are Orthodox jews. That is the Ark," Rothschild pointed to the cabinet, "and contains the Torah scrolls which are the first five books of the Hebrew bible. Over the year the whole of the bible is read in sequence from the Bimah." Rothschild moved his finger to the dais. "Which means high place. Anyway, I'm sure you don't need a lecture. How can we help?"

"Is there a view over the front? I want to be able to see Godwin Road."

"There is. Follow me." Rothschild led Gray and Pfeffer to a set of stairs. A rope barrier stretched across the access. "We don't use up here very much now," he said as he unhitched the rope. The narrow steps took them onto the mezzanine. Beneath Gray could see the dais and across onto the other balcony. Rothschild took Gray to a small window about five feet up the wall. "There." Gray glanced through. Godwin Road was indeed below, but he couldn't see Petrela. The angle was too acute.

"Any other windows with a different view?" asked Gray.

"No, I'm sorry."

Gray leaned over the mezzanine barrier. "What about that?" He pointed to the scaffolding. Standing on the top of it would give someone a view through the dome.

"Maybe."

First the scaffolding needed dragging over. Gray released the wheel brakes. Moving such a large structure, about twenty feet tall, was easier than first appeared. Once he had some momentum the well oiled wheels turned easily. When the scaffolding was beneath the dome Gray reset the brakes then used the ladder to climb. It was only when he was at the top that he felt unsafe. The structure seemed to shift under his weight. Gray wasn't great with heights, even relatively short drops like these freaked him out a little. But he had to see for himself, so he pushed aside his fears as best he could.

The view would do. He could look right down onto Petrela and she was unlikely to be able to see him. The kid was across the road again, a peaked cap low over his eyes. Gray had hoped he would be. He climbed back down.

"Well?" asked Rothschild.

"It'll work," said Gray.

"Are you okay, sir?" asked Pfeffer. "You look a little pale."

"I'm fine. Are you okay to get yourself up there and take photos of everything that moves?"

"Yes, sir."

"Good, then let's rattle a few cages."

Twenty Two

Petrela's head dropped as soon as she saw Gray. She twisted away, ignored him, hunched her shoulders tight. Gray moved around into her eyeline, but she turned her head again, her eyebrows a V of disapproval. Almost childlike in behaviour: if she couldn't see him he wasn't there.

"I'm back, E."

"Piss off, if you know what's good for you," she hissed, burying her hands in her jacket pockets. She glanced across the road, towards the kid Gray had seen previously. He was on his phone still.

Petrela looked at Gray straight on, finally. "I don't want any trouble." The anger was replaced by fear. Her face had turned pale, her eyes wide.

"With who, your boss?"

The kid was watching them both intently now. "I cannot say any more. Please leave, I won't be responsible for you."

"Why?"

"He'll be coming. You should go, *please*."

Petrela started to walk away, but Gray grabbed her at the elbow. She tried to tug free, but his grip was too strong. He didn't want her leaving Pfeffer's viewpoint. "I assume your minder over there has messaged Leka?"

Another look towards the kid. "This is going to be bad for both of us," she said. "You really don't want to mess with him."

Then a car came round the corner at speed, the blue Lexus again. "Oh, shit." Petrela shook Gray off and backed up towards the fence. The kid got up and walked away.

The Lexus screeched to a halt beside Gray. This time Leka got out of the driver seat, alone and without a minder to replace Joseph. He left the door wide open. Leka was chewing on some gum, jaw working fast, fists clenched. He strode over to Petrela, who'd shrunk back against the railings, trying to make herself small and unobtrusive.

"I'm sorry, Leka," she said. "He came up to me."

"What have I told you, stupid bitch?" shouted Leka. Petrela cowered, hands over her face.

"I'm sorry, I'm sorry!"

"Leave her alone," said Gray.

As Leka turned to Gray, Petrela dropped her hands. But Leka twirled fast, backhanded her, catching her on the cheek. She shrieked in pain and fell to the floor, holding her face.

Gray ran at Leka and threw himself at him in a rugby tackle, catching the Albanian at hip height before he could react. Leka hit the pavement hard, Gray on top of him. Leka shoved Gray off. Then positions were reversed, Leka above Gray, throwing punches into Gray's midriff. Leka's yellow teeth were bared, his eyes wide and unblinking. Gray tried to shield himself but Leka's hands were fast and Gray felt searing pain in his side where he was struck once, twice.

"Police! Move away, sir!" The shout came from behind Gray. It was Pfeffer. Leka paused, focused on her. "Now, or I'll use this." She shifted into Gray's eyeline. Pfeffer was holding an aerosol pointed towards the Albanian. It would contain mace.

If she sprayed, Gray would get a faceful too. "Don't move any further. You're under arrest."

Leka held his hands up, got up slowly and backed away. "I'm glad you're here, officer," said Leka. "This man, he attacked me!"

Gray stood, a pain in his kidneys. "You know exactly who I am."

"I swear," said Leka to Pfeffer, "I've never seen him before in my life!"

"Bullshit," said Gray.

"Sir, if you'd do the honours." Pfeffer handed Gray a pair of handcuffs.

"Hands behind your back," said Gray.

Leka allowed his arms to hang loose. Gray spun the Albanian around, pushed him up against the fence, lifted Leka's unresisting arms and ratcheted the handcuffs around his wrists.

"Petrela's done a runner," said Pfeffer.

Gray glanced over his shoulder. "Again." This time they'd be round to wherever she lived and bring her in. But first they needed Leka in custody. "Call the station," said Gray. He kept hold of Leka.

"Already done, sir. They'll be a couple of minutes."

"What happened to you photographing everything, regardless of what occurred?" said Gray.

"I got plenty of footage and I couldn't stand by while you were in trouble."

"I was fine."

In the distance Gray could hear a siren before a police van came hurtling along Godwin Road, lights flashing. Pfeffer stepped into the street and waved. The van bumped up the kerb. Two uniform got out from the front, a man and a woman.

"Take him in," said Gray, pointing to Leka. The movement made Gray wince in pain again. "Book him for assault."

"I haven't done anything," shouted Leka.

The uniform pushed the protesting Leka into the van then departed.

The rabbi was waiting for them at the entrance to the synagogue. "Are you okay?" he asked, handing Pfeffer the camera.

"Fine," said Gray. "Thank you for allowing us to use your place of worship."

"It was my pleasure. I hope you got everything you needed."

"We'll see."

At the car Gray passed Pfeffer the keys. "Can you drive?" Bits of him hurt where Leka's knuckles had gone in.

Once they were moving Pfeffer said, "I'll get an APB out on Peterela when we're back."

"And send a couple of uniform round to where she lives, too. I want a proper word with her, away from her minder."

Twenty Three

Pfeffer entered Gray's office, held out the camera. "In case you want to take a look at the footage, sir. I've already downloaded everything."

"Sure." Gray took the camera. The images Pfeffer would have captured weren't admissible in court and he'd never intended them to be. "I'm going to interview Leka shortly. Want to join me?"

"Wouldn't miss it for the world, sir."

"We're just waiting for his lawyer to arrive."

"I'll have him brought in once he's been fully processed."

Pfeffer left. Gray dry swallowed a couple of paracetamol. His sides ached, but could have been worse. He sat behind his desk and looked at the photos on the camera's rear screen. He flicked through each file. There were photos and video. Several of the shots clearly showed the Albanian's face.

Pfeffer was at Gray's door once more. "We got a hit on his fingerprints," she said. "His surname is Krisniqi."

"Great news." Gray entered the PNC, typed in Krisniqi's name.

Krisniqi had picked up a speeding ticket via a mobile camera team eighteen months ago just outside London. The car he'd been driving at the time was linked to a UK limited company, the details of which were opaque as it was registered in the Cayman Islands. Gray became immediately suspicious. Because this meant the business was a shell and had something to hide.

Krisniqi had resided in the UK for nearly five years. Albania wasn't part of the European Union, where free movement between the 28 member states was allowed. Therefore Krisniqi would have had to apply to enter the country. But Gray couldn't find the request or port entry details. He gave up for now. He'd be speaking to Krisniqi shortly.

IT WAS ALMOST TWO HOURS later when Gray's phone rang. The pain in his kidneys had shrunk to a dull ache. The custody sergeant, Hoyall said, "Krisniqi's lawyer has arrived, Sol. They're in one of the interview rooms, in discussion."

"Let me know when they're done, please," said Gray.

"Will do." Hoyall disconnected.

A further twenty minutes ticked by before Hoyall called once more. "The suspect is ready."

"At bloody last."

"They're in room three, waiting for you."

"On my way." Outside, in the Detectives' Office Gray said to Pfeffer, "Good to go?"

"Absolutely, sir."

They headed to the custody suite. The interview room was sparsely decorated. Magnolia-painted walls, a table, four chairs, a voice recorder and a camera lens in a corner where ceiling met wall. Krisniqi was already seated, a uniformed officer to one side. Adjacent to Krisniqi sat a good-looking man, in his forties, wearing a well cut dark blue suit, white shirt and a red tie.

Gold cufflinks glittered and a monogram, HF, was stitched beside them in the same red as his tie.

"Henry Farrier," said the solicitor, shaking Pfeffer's hand, then Gray's, revealing a pinkie ring. Farrier wasn't a duty solicitor, Gray knew them all, and Farrier was too old to be recently appointed to the bar.

"Do you want me to stay, sir?" asked the uniform of Gray.

"We're fine, thanks." The uniform left. "We haven't met before," said Gray to Farrier.

"You're right, Inspector Gray," deadpanned Farrier. Gray disliked him immediately. "I'm here representing my client."

"Thank you for stating the obvious."

"All part of the job."

Gray started the digital recorder, itemised the names of everyone present, along with the time and date, before turning to the detainee.

"Mr Krisniqi, that's your name, right? Leka Krisniqi?"

"It is," answered Farrier. Krisniqi appeared not to have heard. He was focused on a point on the floor a few feet away.

"Mr Krisniqi, you've been charged with two counts of assault, one of which is against a police officer, contrary to section 89 of the Police Act 1996. You face a sentence of up to 6 months' imprisonment and potentially a fine of up to £5,000. Thereafter the potential of being deported exists."

"My client is aware of and deeply regrets his error of judgement." Farrier made Krisniqi sound like a naughty schoolboy. "Mr Krisniqi has not been in this position previously. He possesses a largely unblemished record, just one minor speeding offence against him."

"I think this is more than an error, Mr Farrier."

The solicitor stared back at Gray. "I conferred with my client before your arrival and Mr Krisniqi intends to plead not guilty to the charges. Mr Krisniqi was fearful for his own life when you confronted him. As I am sure you are aware, hate crime against immigrants is a problem in Thanet and Mr Krisniqi was simply defending himself."

"By hitting a woman?" asked Pfeffer.

"Mr Krisniqi is well aware how stupid his actions were and intends to atone for them."

"Mr Krisniqi knew I was a policeman," said Gray.

"So you stated your position, as a police officer?"

"Not at that time, but Mr Krisniqi and I had met the previous day."

Farrier leant into Krisniqi, who whispered into his ear. "Mr Krisniqi does not deny you met yesterday, but assures me that you did not declare yourself."

"There were witnesses – Mr Krisniqi's driver, Joseph, and Miss Emina Petrela."

"Can you provide written statements from either party?"

"Not at this time," admitted Gray.

Farrier opened his arms wide in a 'what can you do?' gesture. "Unless you have anything else to state I believe my client and I are finished."

"I've further questions."

"We can sit here all day, if you wish, but we won't be able to provide you with any additional information." Farrier smiled again.

"I believe Mr Krisniqi is involved in the supply of illegal class A narcotics into Thanet."

"That is an extremely serious accusation, Inspector Gray. Do you have a shred of evidence to back up your claim?" asked Farrier.

"Our enquiries are proceeding."

"Unless you have direct proof of wrongdoing then I'd suggest this is also mere speculation on your part."

"I'm able to make an offer to Mr Krisniqi."

"I can't see why that would be of interest, inspector, however I will indulge you."

"In return for helping us with our enquiries into drug-smuggling, Kent Police would be prepared to drop the assault charges against Mr Krisniqi."

"Assault charges Mr Krisniqi is denying." Farrier sighed. "Really, inspector? I think we're done."

Gray ended the recording. He had Krisniqi returned to his cell and Farrier left Odell House.

"That didn't go so well," said Pfeffer.

"I'd have been surprised if Krisniqi would have leaked any information about the people above him. Farrier was smooth and well prepared, I admit."

"Maybe we'll have a bit more luck with Petrela."

"I haven't heard whether we've pulled her in, yet," said Gray.

AT THE CUSTODY DESK he said to Sergeant Hoyall, a tall, cadaverous man, "Has Petrela been found?"

"Not to my knowledge. Let me just check in case somebody else handled her." Hoyall tapped away at his computer. "She's not logged."

"Let me know as soon as she is."

"No problem," said Hoyall.

Gray woke his computer and entered an internet search engine. He tapped in 'Henry Farrier lawyer'. A page of results was returned almost immediately. There was a sponsored ad for a local company then beneath a legal firm called Farrier and Balls. Gray clicked on the link.

The company web page was laid out in gold with a black background, tastefully done. Farrier was one of the partners. Another Farrier was listed – an older-looking man who Gray assumed was the father. Under the 'contact us' page were several addresses. The firm had branches in London, Birmingham and Manchester – England's three largest cities.

Gray was intrigued. Why would someone like Krisniqi warrant expensive representation? Seemingly, Krisniqi was only one rung up from Petrela herself. Gray opened up his wallet and pulled out Roza's business card.

Perhaps she knew someone who could help.

Twenty Four

In the middle of the night Gray's mobile bleeped. Gray reached out for it and read the message. Petrela had been found and was in the cells. Gray tried to get some more sleep, but it was no use. He rose more than an hour earlier than he usually did and took a shower before heading into Odell House. His hair still damp, Gray went straight to the custody suite where Hoyall was on duty once again.

"Where was she found?" asked Gray.

"Ramsgate," said Hoyall. "Turned out she was hiding in the tunnels." The tunnels were an old railway route cut into the cliffs just outside the town, between where the junkie Nolan had been found dead and the main sands. "A member of the public discovered her in a right mess and called it in. She was wet, dirty and freezing her arse off. An ambulance got to her first so we arrested her at the hospital and brought her here once she was released. She's been charged with intent to supply Class A drugs. That's what you wanted, right?"

"It'll do. How is she?"

"Other than having a mouth on her, she's fine. No lasting effects from her ordeal." Hoyall rolled his eyes.

"Has she been causing problems?"

"According to the night shift she's been up half the night screaming the usual stuff. That she hadn't done anything, she's not going to talk. Blah, blah, blah."

"Bring her to one of the interview rooms, would you?"

"No problem," said Hoyall. "I'm sure you'll have a delightful time." He grinned.

Gray was waiting when Hoyall and a uniform led Petrela in. Hoyall had a look of fury on his features. A fresh faced man that Gray knew to be one of the newly qualified duty lawyers, called Perry Xander, wandered in behind. Xander was a decent man, but still finding his way, not yet hardened to the practices of defending criminals who habitually lied. Perry was almost too nice for the job. He'd either learn or leave.

"Apologies for the delay sir," said Hoyall through gritted teeth. "Miss Petrela wasn't keen to join you, but we insisted."

Hoyall pressed Petrela into the seat opposite Gray.

"Prick," said Petrela.

Hoyall clenched his fists. "Is that all, sir?"

"Thank you, Sergeant," said Gray. Hoyall nodded and departed, the uniform trailing after him. Petrela twisted her body away so she was at ninety degrees to Gray, her back to Xander. Gray went through the process of declaring his, Xander's and Petrela's presence for the recording before he opened up the interview properly.

"Miss Petrela," said Gray when he was done. "I understand you were rather agitated overnight."

"He tried to touch my arse," said Petrela.

"Who?"

"That guy who brought me in."

"Sergeant Hoyall?"

"I want to complain. He felt me up before his friend came into the cell."

"That's a serious accusation, Miss Petrela," said Gray.

She shrugged. "If you let me out now I'll forget all about it."

"Are you aware we have CCTV – inside and outside each cell?"

Realisation dawned on Petrela's face, like she hadn't known she was being monitored. "It was round by the toilet, where the camera doesn't face. Just release me." But she didn't sound as assured now to Gray.

"Take me through what happened. Were you on the toilet at the time?"

"I was washing my hands."

"Then what?"

"He came in and ... touched me."

"Can you confirm where?"

Petrela stood, bent slightly at the waist, reached around and smacked her backside loud enough for it to sound like a slap. She sat, glared at Gray.

He said, "Miss Petrela has just indicated she was touched on the right cheek of her buttocks."

Petrela nodded, with more conviction. "That's correct."

"So, you're saying when we review the footage we'll find Sergeant Hoyall entering your cell while you're at the sink and he comes over to you?"

"Yes."

"Okay then. We'll suspend the interview while we do so. Although I have to warn you, Miss Petrela, that falsely accusing a police officer is an offence in itself." Gray reached out for the recorder.

Petrela hunched over, arms on her thighs. "I can't stay here. He'll think I'm talking."

"Who, Krisniqi?" asked Gray. Petrela reminded Gray of Stretch. More the way he'd behaved than how she appeared.

"He didn't do anything," said Petrela quietly.

"Could you repeat that, Miss Petrela?"

"I said," louder this time, "I made it up, about that cop touching my arse."

"So you don't want us to follow up on your complaint? You wish to withdraw the accusation? You're saying you lied?"

Petrela nodded, not looking at Gray.

"Why?"

"I want out, now. I *need* to be out."

"Sergeant Hoyall said you were shouting half the night. Why?" Petrela shrugged. Gray continued, "I think I know. You were trying to get a message over to Mr Krisniqi who's in one of the nearby cells. He would have heard you. I don't believe you're angry, you're scared."

"Yes, yes!"

"Okay, let's start again, shall we?"

"I'm not telling you anything."

"Yesterday, Mr Krisniqi attacked you."

"He didn't."

"I saw him slap you round the face."

"I don't remember."

"Clearly, you're lying." Petrela stared at the floor. "What I find interesting, Miss Petrela," continued Gray, "is the difference in representation between you and Mr Krisniqi. No offence to your solicitor here, but he comes for free." Xander nodded at Gray to indicate none taken. "Whereas the lawyer acting for Mr Krisniqi is high end. I'd like to know about our friend."

Petrela swivelled around to face Gray at last. She placed her forearms on the table, cuffs in clear view. "Look," she said, "if they think I've been helping you the cost is too great, all right? These people, they don't ask questions like you. They just make decisions. I have to look out for myself and my family. I don't want anybody to suffer." Petrela's face had sagged. She appeared on the verge of tears. This wasn't an act.

"What family?"

"Nobody you can help." Petrela shook her head. "If you're going to charge me, do it." She sat back in her chair.

"Is one of your relatives in trouble?" Nothing from her. "Miss Petrela," said Gray. "I can't help if you don't speak with me."

"Talking to you is the worst thing I can do. Why won't you understand?" Petrela stood, went to the door, faced it.

Xander shrugged.

"Okay," said Gray. Outside in the corridor the same uniform who'd escorted Petrela here was leaning against the wall. "Take Miss Petrela back to her cell please."

Petrela was unresisting and flaccid when she was led away. She glanced over her shoulder at Gray, tears in her eyes. Then, as if a switch had been flipped, she screamed, "Fucking cops! You'll get nothing out of me!"

Twenty Five

Gray pushed the interview room door closed and answering his ringing phone.

"I'm sorry, it took a little longer than I'd first assumed," said Roza. "I had to pull in some favours."

"Not too many, I hope."

"I contacted my brother's best friend. Strictly it's him who used up the favours. First, Petrela. She was born in Kukes in the north east of the country, about 60 miles from Tirana, which is the country's capital." Gray remembered from Petrela's record. "Kukes is near the border with Kosovo. It is a beautiful place, but can be dangerous sometimes, partly because it is poor and partly because of its location. Petrela did well at school and went to University in Tirana to study engineering, then she suddenly dropped out near the end of her first year."

"When was this?"

"Just over twelve months ago. She simply disappeared. I've emailed through the most recent photograph I could access, pulled from a social media account."

"Well, somehow she got herself to the UK. Does she have a police record in Albania?"

"None."

"Very strange because here she's a drug dealer. I wonder what happened in between?"

"I can't help you with that."

"And Krisniqi?"

"In an interesting coincidence, he's from Kukes too."

"Did they know each other?"

"Not that I can see. Krisniqi is a good fifteen years older. Leka translates as *defender of men* which is quite apt."

"Why?"

"Because my brother's friend believes Krisniqi is a *Mik*."

"Remind me what a *Mik* is?"

"The *Mik* is the right hand man to the gang leader, the *Kryetar*. The *Mik* liaises with the gang members and is responsible for coordinating all the unit activities and reporting back to the *Kryetar* who is the underling of the *Krye* or boss."

"So he's pretty senior."

"He's the second highest ranking person in the local network, so I would agree that Krisniqi is not your basic foot soldier. I will send you his file if you wish."

"Please. And thank you. This is really helpful."

"That isn't all, Solomon." Roza's voice had dropped to barely a whisper. "Krisniqi has a number of known associates. There is one in particular. His name is Arian Prifti; but that is not his birth name. That has been lost. Prifti is a *Kryetar*.

"Prifti has several honorifics, the ones he goes by the most are *The Priest*, or *The Golden Priest*. Prifti has made a lot of money, which is where 'golden' comes from. 'Priest' is because of his religious belief. It is more than likely that if Krisniqi is around, then Prifti is too. If you really want to hurt the Albanian network, Solomon, then you cut off the snake's head. You can get to Prifti through Krisniqi. Use one to bring down the other."

It was a good strategy.

Roza drew in a deep breath, like she was preparing for something. "I want to put in a request to DI Yarrow that I be seconded to your investigation," she said.

"Why, Roza?"

"Because Prifti may have been involved in the murder of my brother. It's possible he might even have pulled the trigger."

"Jesus." Gray put his head in his hand. "Does Yarrow know about Prifti?"

"I have told only you."

"I'm not sure, Roza. You might be too close to all of this to be objective."

"Solomon, I am asking you as someone who feels what it is like to lose a close relative, who has to find out the truth."

"Why do you believe I'm so predictable?" asked Gray.

"We have a mutual friend in London – Marcus Pennance." Pennance was a DI in the Sapphire Unit. He and Gray had worked together unofficially to try and find Gray's missing son, Tom. And Pennance had been involved in Pivot. Roza continued, "So I am aware that you will sometimes bend the rules to reach the answers." Roza sounded like Sylvia now.

"I'll need to clear this with Hamson first."

"You don't. You already know whether you want my help or not."

"I need at least a semi-plausible reason for bringing you on board."

"I've thought of that. I can be both an expert close to hand and a translator. If you or DCI Hamson are concerned about budget I will pay my own expenses. We can say it is being charged to Pivot."

Given Gray's own experiences, how could he say no? "Okay, I'll make it happen."

"Thank you, Solomon." Roza's relief was obvious down the phone. "You will not regret your decision. I will be down today."

"That's fast."

"I have already cleared up all my affairs and packed a bag in the expectation that you would agree." Gray laughed. "I have booked Albion again, where we met the first time."

A thought occurred to Gray. "Don't do that. I've a spare bedroom. You can stay with me at my flat. I'll drive you into the station every day. It'll be cheaper."

"No thank you. I'd prefer the hotel."

"If you're sure?"

"I like my own space. But as a compromise you can still drive me if you wish."

"Works for me. Take the train down to Margate and I'll pick you up. Just let me know when you're arriving."

"See you soon," said Roza and disconnected.

Gray opened his email, clicked on the note Roza had sent him, then on the file attachment. "Good God," he said when Petrela's photo popped up. She looked very different. No tattoos, a neat hairstyle – blonde tresses hanging past her shoulders and a sharp fringe. She was smiling and seemed happy, a natural image. Nothing like she was now. As he'd said to Roza, something happened to Petrela that had changed her. But what?

He called Emily Wyatt.

"Hi," she said when she answered. "How's things?"

"Non stop," said Gray. "Just ringing to see if you'd heard anything about Lowther at the NCA?"

"God, yes, I have. Sorry, I meant to call but it's been stupidly busy here too, wrapping up Pivot. We should be done in a couple of weeks at the most."

"No need to apologise, I understand."

"Anyway, your Mr Lowther is an intriguing man. You could almost call him famous within his own circle."

"How so?"

"He's ex-undercover, though most of the work he undertook is classified, records heavily redacted. Apparently he brought down some powerful criminals. His skill was working his way into drug gangs all over the country. He can be volatile and and has been known to break the rules, but a friend told me management liked the results he produced so let it slide. These days he's no longer undercover, the stress got too much. Lowther got himself into and out of a couple of tight spots – he's been put in hospital several times and threatened with a gun. He may be suffering post traumatic stress disorder. That's why he was pulled from working in the field. Now he's a handler."

"Jesus."

"Right, very different to our experiences," said Wyatt. "That's all I was able to learn."

"It's enough, thanks Emily."

"You can buy me dinner, how about that as recompense?"

"Deal."

"See you soon." Wyatt disconnected.

Gray sat back. There were still plenty of holes. Key to everything seemed to be the man he was holding in the cells – Leka Krisniqi. He made a decision.

It could be risky, but sometimes you had to break a few eggs…

Twenty Six

"You've done what?" asked Hamson. She'd stood, was leaning over her desk, knuckles down.

"Let him go," said Gray.

"I bloody heard the first time."

"So why ask me?"

"Because I didn't think an officer of mine could be so stupid."

"Von, we weren't going to learn anything with Krisniqi in custody."

"But we were holding a senior man in a potentially major crime organisation."

"Who was being represented by a top lawyer, wasn't saying anything, doesn't have any outstanding warrants for his arrest and whose assault victim is refusing to press charges."

"We could have charged him without Petrela's say so, you know that."

"And he'd have been off the streets for a couple of months, at best. Probably not even that."

"What's to say he won't move somewhere else?"

Gray remembered Krisniqi's smug grin when he'd been told he was being released with just a caution. He was untouchable. "Trust me, he's staying put."

"I hope you're right, Sol."

"Roza Selimi is arriving soon to support our enquiries."

"Since when?"

"We need help, you heard what Yarrow said."

"And he's okay with losing his resident expert?"

"Pivot is winding down." Gray was careful not to answer Hamson's question directly.

"Who's picking up her tab?"

"Not us." Which was truthful, at least. "Look, there's something big going on we've barely uncovered. The Albanians are a group of people you and I have virtually no experience of."

Hamson sat down. Gray took a seat too. "That's valid." Her mobile rang. She said, "Marsh, I'd better take this."

As Gray was closing Hamson's door his own mobile vibrated. Boughton, the beat cop. "Damian, how's things?" asked Gray.

"I hope you're happy." Boughton sounded anything but.

"I don't understand."

"There's a body been found. You should see it."

"Where?"

"Norfolk Road," said Boughton, then disconnected. Gray slowly removed the phone from his ear.

"Oh, God," he said.

Twenty Seven

An ambulance was waiting outside the property. Paramedics were in the process of unloading a gurney, attempting to avoid the dustbins which still spilled out from the front garden onto the pavement, but nobody was hurrying.

Gray showed his warrant card to one of the paramedics who was young, tall and bearded, and said, "Can you give me a few minutes to look over the scene before you remove him?"

"Sure," replied the paramedic. "He's not going anywhere."

"Thanks."

"I'll warn you though. It's not pleasant, he's been dead a day or more."

"I'll survive."

The paramedic switched off from Gray, leant against the back of the ambulance and fell into conversation with his female colleague. She held out a packet of cigarettes and the bearded man took one.

A uniformed police constable stood at the front entrance. "Evening, sir. Up on the second floor," he said. "You can't miss the smell. That's what alerted his neighbours."

As Gray headed inside he heard the PC inform his colleague of Gray's arrival over his Airwave radio. The stairs still creaked under Gray's feet, there remained an odour of damp in the air. The other uniform stood beside the door into the flat. Once, long ago, it had been painted black but now it was marked and scuffed, the gloss faded. The uniform nodded at Gray as he entered.

Within was decay and excrement. The space was a single room. A space an estate agent would call a studio comprising of a tiny kitchen area and a bed. Dirty crockery filled the sink. Gray didn't bother to investigate, someone else would have done that already.

The bed was a double. On top lay the body. Gray got nearer, the stench growing stronger as he did so. It was hot, like the radiator was on full blast. Stretch was lying on his back, sheets clenched between his fists, head rearwards on a strained neck. Gray shifted his gaze upwards to get a better look at the face. Eyes squeezed shut, teeth bared, as if he'd been in extreme pain at the moment he passed. Another overdose, making twenty deaths now.

Gray put his head in his hands, hoping it hadn't been his actions which had led to Stretch's death. Gray remembered what Boughton had said before he terminated the call.

I hope you're happy...

WHEN GRAY RETURNED to the station he was anything but happy.

He paused in the centre of the Detectives' Office. "Everyone," he said. "I need a minute." Faces turned to him, curiosity playing on their features. "Who attended the overdose of a man on Norfolk Road earlier today?"

Pfeffer raised her hand. "That would be me, sir."

"Come into my office, please. The rest of you, back to your work." Gray shrugged off his jacket as Pfeffer joined him. "Close the door would you?"

Pfeffer did and Gray pointed to the chair in front of his desk. No room for a separate conference table like Hamson. Gray hung up his jacket, sat down himself.

"What can I do for you, sir?" asked Pfeffer.

"I wanted to get your impression of the scene."

Pfeffer thought for a moment, her eyeballs lifting upwards and to the left as she unconsciously accessed her memory, before she focused on Gray again. "Nothing remarkable, sir. Appeared to be an overdose and he obviously died in significant pain."

"Yes," said Gray, feeling another twinge of guilt. "How did you pick up the case?"

Pfeffer pulled a face. "Just timing, sir."

"Tell me the truth, please."

"DC Worthington refused to attend, sir. He said it was 'just another dead junkie and not worth our time.'"

"Christ sake."

"That's one way of putting it, sir."

"One more thing, Melanie."

"Sir?"

"Stop calling me sir all the time when it's just you and me, all right?"

Pfeffer grinned. "No problem."

Pfeffer left Gray alone. He received a text from Roza Selimi, telling him when she was arriving.

Gray's internal phone rang as he pressed send on his reply. It was the custody sergeant, Hoyall. "Sol, what's happening with Petrela? Are you letting her loose or are you going to charge her with something?"

Gray had forgotten about Petrela. "I'm on my way down."

GRAY WAITED WHILE HOYALL unlocked the heavy metal door. When it swung back, Petrela was standing against the far wall as inmates were taught to do so in prison when warders entered. She was biting the nails of a finger.

"Turn that off, please." Gray pointed to the CCTV camera in the corner of the cell. "I'll be five minutes."

"Okay," said Hoyall. "Bang on the door when you're ready to come out." Hoyall left.

"I'm not talking to you," shouted Petrela before the door closed.

"Krisniqi has been released."

She sagged, flopped down onto the cot next to her. "What do you want?" she sounded and looked drained. She lay back, put an arm over her eyes, as if trying to sleep.

"What I want is information on Krisniqi and his friends. How they operate, where they work out of. Things like that."

Petrela gave a humourless laugh. "You have to be kidding."

"In exchange I'm willing to potentially offer you a place on the witness protection scheme. It would mean a fresh start somewhere well away from Thanet with a new identity." She dropped her arm, turned her head to stare at Gray. "I'm serious."

"So are they. I cannot do it."

"This is a one-chance offer."

Petrela rubbed her eyes. "There's not just me to think about."

"Who?" asked Gray. Petrela shook her head. "We'll put Krisniqi away."

"Can you give me a complete guarantee everybody would be safe?" Gray didn't answer. "That's what I thought."

"Nothing's absolute."

"If you had given me your word I wouldn't have believed you anyway. I know these people. They don't piss around."

"Give me something, E." Petrela swung her legs off the bed, sat hunched over. "Nobody will know it's come from you, that I can promise."

"You won't use this against me?"

"Our conversation never happened."

Petrela stared at Gray for a long moment. "I hate him, I want you to know that. He's the worst person I've ever met. Krisniqi doesn't feel anything for me, I've been just a whore or a punch bag depending on how he felt at the time. Something amusing to play with when he's bored. And there's nothing I can do about it. That's why I got these tattoos." She pointed to her neck. "To put him off the sex at least. It worked, but he turned his attention elsewhere."

Gray said, "You mentioned family when we spoke earlier. Is that it?" Petrela shook her head. "Help me."

"No."

"Even the smallest piece of information might make the difference."

"How do I know I can trust you?"

"The cameras are off, remember?"

Petrela closed her eyes, fell silent for a long moment. "There's been an interruption in the drug supply recently."

"How do the drugs normally come in?"

"By truck from the continent. The guy who handles the shipments hasn't been around. It's been driving Krisniqi crazy. He's ranted about it several times."

It was a long shot. Gray remembered Langham telling him he dealt with Eastern Europe, including Albania, and Myerscough had disappeared. "Is the guy called Myerscough?"

"I've no idea. That's not the sort of thing he'd tell me."

"But you recognised the photo I showed you."

"Maybe."

"He's Myerscough."

Petrela stood. "That's all, I can't do anymore."

"E," said Gray.

Petrela cut him off. "I said, we're done." She stood, banged on the door.

"If you think of anything else, I'd appreciate it if you could let me know," said Gray as keys rattled in the lock.

"Won't be happening." Petrela moved over to the toilet. "I need a piss, so if you'd excuse me."

Hoyall opened up. Worthington was standing in the corridor a few yards away.

"When do we have to let her go?" asked Gray once the cell door was locked.

Hoyall checked his watch. "About forty-five minutes."

"Kick her out now then."

"Will do."

Worthington fell into step beside Gray heading back to the Detective's Office. "Anything from Petrela?" he asked.

"Not a bloody word," said Gray.

"You were in there an age for nothing."

"Checking up on me now are you?"

Worthington laughed. "No, sir. Just keen to make progress. I hoped Petrela might be a breakthrough."

"I don't see her being of any use at all," lied Gray.

"Pity, anyway, I'm going to shake the snake." Worthington pointed at the door to the gents toilets a few yards in front.

"Too much information for my liking."

Worthington grinned and entered the bathroom as they passed. Gray turned around and retraced his steps. Hoyall was at the custody desk, filling in some paperwork.

Hoyall looked up at Gray's approach. "Forgotten something, sir?"

"How long was Worthington hanging around outside the cell?"

The sergeant frowned. "Most of the time you were with Petrela, I think. Why?"

"He should have better things to be doing, is all. I'll have a word with him later." Gray left Hoyall. Why was Worthington was so interested in Petrela?

Gray couldn't come up with a legitimate reason.

Twenty Eight

Gray was heading into work for the start of his shift the following day when his phone rang.

"Morning, Sol." The voice of Ben Clough came out of the car's speakers and filled the interior.

"Hey, Ben. How's things?"

"Can you come by the hospital? There's something I'd like to talk to you about." The pathologist, a serious man at the best of times, sounded dour.

"Sure, when?"

"Is now okay?"

"That urgent?" Gray tried to inject some amusement into his voice. The attempt fell on stony ground.

"Yes, it is. I wouldn't ask otherwise."

"I'll see you in a few minutes."

Gray's normal commute from Broadstairs to Odell House took him right by the QEQM hospital on the Margate Road. Soon, Gray passed the sprawling mix of Victorian and not so new modern buildings on his left. He turned into the car park, found a spot, bought a ticket and threw it on his dashboard. He loathed that he was forced to pay to park to use a public facility. Worse, none of the revenue went to the hospital, instead a private firm took the money.

He found Clough seated behind his desk in his office near the pathology suite. The room was tiny and box-shaped. Barely enough leeway for a desk, two visitors chairs and a book case. Certificates of accomplishment hung behind Clough's desk. Light flooded into the room from long, narrow windows inset high up and along one wall.

Clough stood when Gray entered, not out of courtesy, but expediency, giving room for Gray to get himself in. Clough was a thin, wiry and sensitive man. Recently, he'd started wearing reading glasses, round and rimmed with a brass-coloured metal. Clough held out his hand to shake, which Gray took. As usual, Clough's hands were cold to the touch.

"What's so pressing?" asked Gray as he took a seat.

"These." Clough tapped a stack of paperwork by his elbow. Gray picked up the top folder. It was a medical record, for Archie Nolan, the overdose which had started everything. Gray flicked through the documentation, but didn't really know what he was looking at so handed it back. "They're the drug deaths that have occurred in the last six months. Twenty of them." So Stretch was included.

"I don't understand, Ben."

"All of these poor people died as a result of heroin. However, twelve of them, including Nolan, took drugs which were cut with Fentanyl. It's an opioid that's a hundred times more powerful than morphine and very cheap."

Gray had heard of opioids, they were a major problem in the US at the moment, with thousands of people a year dying over there. Patients, taking opiods for legitimate reasons, often became hooked on the addictive drugs and when their prescription ended they still needed the hit. But medical grade opioids were expensive, creating a gap in the market which the cartels exploited, manufacturing their own low cost versions and producing an epidemic in the process. Thankfully, opioid abuse in the UK was comparatively rare.

Clough continued, "Even a really small amount, just a couple of milligrammes, the weight of a snowflake, is fatal. The analysis found comparatively five times that amount was taken by these people."

"So, anyone who had a hit like that would die?" asked Gray.

"One hundred per cent. Once the drug was in their bodies there was no coming back."

"Good God." Stretch had been right: users were being murdered.

"And it would be an extremely painful way to go. It was only when you requested follow-up analyses I began looking properly. I'm sorry."

"Ben, everybody missed it. The key thing now is to make sure no more deaths happen."

Gray picked up Nolan's PM report once more. The data inside still meant nothing to him, but he felt he had some answers now. "What about Stretch?"

"Who?"

"Sorry, Dean Mold."

"Ah yes, my most recent guest. I rushed his analysis through. His was a normal concoction, if that's what it can be called. The heroin had been heavily cut with cornstarch."

"So, he's not one of your twelve?"

"No," said Clough. Gray was glad he was sitting down because suddenly he felt weak with relief. He hadn't been responsible for Stretch's death after all. "These are your unfortunate victims." Clough handed over a piece of paper, names printed upon it.

Twenty Nine

Gray found Damian Boughton on a break. The beat cop was sitting in a corner of the station canteen by himself with a part-eaten bacon sandwich and a glass of water.

"Mind if I join you?" asked Gray.

"Free country," said Boughton, as if spending any time with Gray was the last thing he wanted.

Gray dragged out a chair. Boughton eyed him as he sat, took a bite out of his sandwich. Gray let Boughton chew and swallow. "I've just met with Clough. The tox report on Stretch showed he died by his own hand from an overdose. Neither you nor I had any involvement."

"I know," nodded Boughton. "Which is why you're not on your back right now after taking my fist in your teeth."

"How did you find out?"

"I've worked here a long while, Sol." Boughton held his sandwich up. "Is that all? Or can I get on with this?"

"I'm here to ask for your help."

"After the last time? You've got to be joking."

"I want to find this guy." Gray slid a photo across the table.

Boughton put out a finger, dragged the image closer. He bent to look and took another bite of his sandwich.

"Leka Krisniqi, he's Albanian and I believe he's very senior in the local drug scene. He's part of the structure that's been killing all the junkies recently. Certainly the stuff Stretch bought came from the Albanians." Gray had seen him buy the hit from Petrela. When Stretch passed by Gray's car he'd been walking to his death. "I'd like you to ask your contacts on the street to learn where this guy spends his time hanging out. I'm going to rattle the tree and see what falls out."

"Doing what Solomon Gray does best." Boughton smiled, but without mirth. "Causing trouble."

"I've been taking some advice from an expert on Albanian gangs. She's coming in to work with me shortly."

"You're taking this seriously then?"

"Of course, Damian. Why wouldn't I?"

"As you said yourself, some in your team think it's just junkie scum dying." Boughton finished his sandwich, drained the glass of water. He wiped his fingers on a paper napkin. "I've seen him around."

"Really?" Gray was surprised.

"You're not the only cop. I've been sniffing about. I wasn't aware of his name, though. He operates out of the snooker hall in Cliftonville."

"I know the place."

"Good luck." Boughton pushed back his chair and left without a backward glance.

Thirty

Gray waited on the platform for Roza Selimi's arrival. Wind whistled along the tracks, blowing rubbish in its path. The London train drew to a slow halt, brakes a highpitch squeal as metal gripped metal, the sound cutting through Gray.

A burst of air expelled from the hydraulic brakes once the train finally stopped. There was a repetitive bleeping sound from inside the carriages, the double doors popped and slid apart. This was the end of the tracks for the London route, or the start if you were heading into the capital, so everybody on board got off. Most made for the exit in a small stream. One, a short woman with long dark hair, trailing a suitcase on wheels, paused and looked around.

Gray made his way over. "Hi, Roza."

Roza broke into a smile. "Inspector, thank you for meeting me."

"The least I can do."

"Let me take your bag."

"I'm fine."

"My car's outside."

Gray led Roza into the relative shelter of the entrance hall. Constructed in Victorian times, it was parquet floor beneath a tall, curved roof and a grand clock to let commuters know quite how delayed the service was. As they exited, heavy wooden doors shuttered behind them.

A handful of parking spaces directly out front were all full. Gray's car was up on the kerb, ignoring the double yellows. He opened the boot and Roza placed her case inside. "Did you have a good journey?" asked Gray.

"Draining," said Roza. "Your trains are always full and often late."

"They're a national embarrassment, frankly." Gray got into the driver's seat, started the engine. When the wheels were rolling and they were in the shadow of Arlington House, a high rise right on the sea front, Gray said, "Are you too tired for a bit of work?"

Roza switched her attention from the sea view to Gray. "What are you thinking of?"

"Meeting Leka Krisniqi."

"Solomon, do you not remember what we discussed over dinner just a few days ago? Why do you want to poke the snake?"

"It's the only way I know."

"Trouble lies that way."

Rather than turning at the clock tower roundabout towards Odell House Gray went straight over, leaving the lights of the Dreamland amusement arcade behind.

THE SNOOKER CLUB WAS just off Northdown Road, the artery which ran through Cliftonville and the main shopping area outside of the shopping centre in the New Town. The stores reflected the demographics developing in Thanet – a Polski Slep, bargain booze, several bookies, various takeaways and a cash converters.

The building Gray wanted was about halfway along the busy road on a corner plot. Once it had been the crown jewel in a chain of seaside department stores called Bobby's, started in Margate during the late 1800s, but the founder sold out to a much larger brand before they in turn closed Bobby's in the early 1970's and the town lost another cultural icon – unfortunately by no means the last. Downstairs was now a European supermarket, the large windows blanked off with gaudy prints of the goods they sold. The floor above was white stucco and a domed tower, like a turret.

Gray turned into a side road, drove past a twenty-four-hour gym. He found a spot to park about a hundred yards along. You're insisting we do this then?"

"I am."

"It could be a very bad idea."

"Maybe. You can stay in the car if you prefer."

"I'll come, as long as you agree to one condition."

"Okay."

"If I ask that we leave then we do so."

"All right."

"Do you promise?"

"I promise."

"Please don't make me regret this."

Gray remembered Boughton saying something similar. "I won't." He hoped he was right.

Adjacent to the gym was a double-glazed door and a picnic bench. There wasn't a sign for the snooker hall; all that remained was the fixing. A couple of empty pint glasses sat on the bench and the ash tray was full.

Gray pushed at the unlocked door. He took the stairs directly in front, Roza in his wake. The flight was narrow, the walls scratched and scraped, like someone had dragged something almost too large up or down the stairway.

The stairs emerged in one corner of the first floor. The snooker hall opened up into a space with a high ceiling, sizeable enough for half a dozen of the twelve foot by six foot standard tables. The air was filled with the fug of cigarette smoke and the click of cue striking snooker balls. Otherwise the place was hushed, like a church to the sport. Any conversation came in low overtones. Strip lights suspended directly over the tables, brightly illuminated the green baize, otherwise darkness.

The only other pocket of clarity was a bar in the opposite corner where a handful of people gathered, the area delineated from the rest of the hall by two unoccupied pool tables. Gray made his way between the snooker tables, looking for Krisniqi. Men playing paused as Gray and Roza passed, like they were some strange, confusing, out-of-place beings. Gray caught sight of Krisniqi, leaning on the counter and looking over his shoulder. Behind the bar a heavily tattooed younger man, his hair shaved tight to his skull, in maybe his early 30s, polished a glass.

"We should leave, Solomon," said Roza.

Krisniqi turned, stood tall, arms loose at his side. "This members club," he said, "and men only."

Gray pulled out his warrant card, held it up. "And this provides me and my colleague the right to go where I wish." Krisniqi ignored Gray's card. "Where's the manager?" asked Gray. "Smoking inside is banned and you're breaking the law." The barman pulled a pint and placed it beside Krisniqi's near-empty glass.

"And what is the penalty, Inspector. A slap on the wrist?" Krisniqi picked up his drink, drained what was left and walked over to Roza who was concentrating on her mobile. "Who is this, your sister?" Krisniqi looked Roza up and down, seeming to Gray as if he was inspecting a prize. "Or maybe your mother?" Roza ignored him, still intent on the screen. Krisniqi spoke in his own language, saying something Gray couldn't comprehend. Roza looked up, a blank expression, as if she didn't understand either. Krisniqi said something else, then backed away.

"Solomon," said Roza. Gray ignored her.

"Is that all you are here for?" asked Krisniqi. "To talk about cigarettes and bring me a woman to insult?"

"I'm letting you know I'm coming for you, Krisniqi. People are dying and you're responsible."

Krisniqi opened his arms wide in innocence. "I don't know what you're talking about, inspector." Krisniqi nudged his chin forward. "And neither do they."

Gray turned. The snooker players were assembled in a loose group the other side of the pool tables. Each held a cue in their hands.

Roza's face was pale. She mouthed, "Please."

Krisniqi spoke in a louder voice, "Are you going to have a word with everyone here?" Then Krisniqi spoke in his own language and the men laughed. When Gray didn't answer Krisniqi smirked. "I suggest you walk out now and take your whore with you."

"Solomon," said Roza, quietly, "please, let's go."

"Listen to your woman," said Krisniqi. He picked up the fresh pint and drank.

"Okay," said Gray.

He walked up to the crowd of men, Roza behind him. The men didn't move.

"Let them leave," said Krisniqi.

Reluctantly, the group parted, allowing Gray and Roza a narrow passage. Gray could feel their eyes on him all the way across the hall.

"Come back again, inspector," shouted Krisniqi when Gray was reaching for the door handle.

When they were outside Gray said, "I'm sorry, Roza. That didn't quite go as planned."

Roza said nothing, she wouldn't even look at Gray. He drove back past the club. Nobody was outside to eyeball him as he went by. When they reached Odell House Gray signed Roza in and she clipped her visitor's badge onto a trouser pocket. He led her into the corridors and to the Detectives' Office.

"My office is there." Gray pointed.

Roza nodded, still not speaking.

Gray headed over to check in with Pfeffer. When he passed by Worthington's desk the Geordie stood. "Who's that?" asked Worthington, nodding towards Gray's office.

"Roza, she's helping me out with the Albanians."

"Foreign then?"

"Albanian herself. Why?"

"Cute." Worthington straightened his tie. "I may ask her out. Show her the local sights."

"I doubt she'll be here long enough to fall for your dubious charms."

"That's what they all say." Worthington threw Gray a broad grin.

Gray squatted down beside Pfeffer's desk. Pfeffer raised a questioning eyebrow. "She's called Roza Selimi and she's going to help us get Krisniqi," said Gray.

"I hope she's staying in a hotel?"

"Of course, why?" Pfeffer shrugged, didn't answer. "Any further updates on Myerscough?"

"Nothing sir, though I have been looking at the area where Myerscough was last seen. It's pretty desolate."

"Maybe there's a hut or something where he's holed up."

"I don't get why, though."

"We probably won't until we speak to him."

"There haven't been any responses to the APB. No sightings at the airports, shops, anywhere. Maybe he's still in the marshland?"

"It's possible, I suppose."

"Sir, your guest is looking for you." Roza was outside Gray's office.

"I'll be back in a minute."

Roza went inside as Gray approached. She turned on him. "What were you thinking?"

"I'm sorry." He closed the door.

"We could have disappeared and nobody would have known. And you broke your promise."

"If we'd have left immediately we wouldn't have learned anything."

"And what did you *learn* from the experience?"

"Not much," admitted Gray.

"Well I did," said Roza. "Almost immediately." Roza held out her phone. "Do you remember this man?"

There was a partially blurry image on her screen. "That's the barman from the snooker hall."

"Correct."

Gray had paid him barely any attention. "He just seemed to be keeping his head down."

"I knew him straight away. This man is The Golden Priest, Arian Prifti."

"Your brother's killer?"

"Yes, he's the *Kryetar*, the local big boss running everything. He's here." Roza's face fell. "But we'll never get near him."

"We just did."

"Not close enough."

"You should have told me straight away."

"And what would you have done? Arrested him? We were outnumbered. Men are like fish, Solomon. The great devour the small."

"I've no intention of being devoured."

"Then you need another more sublte way to reach Krisniqi and Prifti."

"Myerscough," said Gray.

Thirty One

"We need to find Jasper Myerscough," said Gray.

"Suddenly Sylvia's husband is important?"

"He might be involved with the Albanians."

"How?"

"I'm not entirely sure. However," Gray held up a hand, ticked his point off one by one on his fingers, "Myerscough works for a haulage company that regularly brings in freight from Europe. The owner, a Mr Langham, says one of the countries they operate with is Albania."

"Bit of a stretch. I'd bet there are many haulage firms who've business out that way."

"That's not all." Another finger. "I've heard separately from a local dealer and one of her junkie customers that gear is in short supply, there's been an interruption to the channel."

"Good, means we're doing our jobs."

"Their problem started about the time Myerscough disappeared. The same dealer sort of confirmed it was Myerscough who's the key link between the gang and the suppliers."

"Sort of?"

"She wouldn't totally commit. Maybe Myerscough was helping get the drugs through without detection or he was working with someone at the port who was doing so, then he was the onward distributor?"

Hamson sat back. "I must say, I'm not convinced by the connection."

"It's the best we've got right now."

"Where's Myerscough then?"

"We have footage showing him disappearing into the marshland below Minster with a backpack."

"He could just have been travelling through."

"Why, though? He'd have to cross acres and acres of bog to reach a road when he'd have driven along a perfectly good dual carriageway to reach Minster. And there's a train station. I think he's still in the marshland, which is why I need some manpower to search the area."

"Bloody hell, the marshland must be a couple of miles in area!"

"About right." Maybe more.

"Are you *certain* that's where he is?"

"It's a decent theory."

"And you want me to release people to run around on a probable wild goose chase?" Hamson shook her head, answered before Gray could. "I'm sorry, no."

"Von..."

Hamson cut Gray off. "We don't have the spare bodies." She held her hand up, palm out, when Gray opened his mouth. "No more discussion. We're done talking. That's my decision for now. Bring me something concrete and I'll maybe reconsider."

"You're wrong," said Gray.

Hamson's expression hardened, the V forming between her down-turned eyebrows. "Way to go on influencing me, inspector." She pointed a single finger. "The door's that way."

Gray left.

"How did it go?" asked Pfeffer when he entered the Detectives' Office.

"As expected," said Gray.

"How many are going to help us search?"

"None."

"Oh."

"Which means it's down to you, me and Roza."

Thirty Two

Pfeffer pulled up on Marsh Farm Road in Minster, a narrow thoroughfare with just enough room for two cars to squeeze by, stopping outside the house where Myerscough was caught on video. Pfeffer let Gray and Roza out first before she manouvered the car tight up against a wall.

Gray stood in view of the front door where the video doorbell was fixed. He then looked up the long, arrow-straight road towards the train station from where Myerscough would have walked. The car park was hidden behind a bank of trees. A few hundred yards along were the railway tracks they'd crossed; the barriers, two red and white striped poles up and standing to attention, the train-approaching warning lights unlit.

"Do you want to speak to the home owner?" asked Pfeffer when she joined them.

"I don't see the need. What are they going to tell us?"

"I suppose so." Pfeffer, dressed for hiking, in walking boots, leggings and wearing a waterproof jacket, handed him a rucksack that had been in the boot of the car. Gray was more casual, in jeans and his warmest coat. Roza's gear was new; she'd been shopping before they set off.

"Let's get going." Gray slung the pack over his shoulder.

They headed south, away from Minster. According to Gray's Ordnance Survey map, the distance to the end of the road was almost a mile. Bushes growing either side of the road obscured the view across the land either side until they reached the gate that allowed access onto the marsh.

Gray paused where the flat vista opened up. He pulled a pair of binoculars from his rucksack and scanned the area. He didn't know this region at all. He wasn't a bird watcher or a walker – there wasn't much of a reason to come here otherwise. All he'd been able to do in advance was study the map and check out photograpghs online.

"Where do we start?" asked Pfeffer.

Gray didn't have a clue, but wasn't going to say. He consulted the map. The marshland formed a rough L shape, with the long side of the letter lying horizontally and the rest pointing down. Minster was to the north while the A299, which Gray had taken to Dover and Langham's the other day, formed the eastern boundary, with Sandwich at the uppermost tip. To the west was the A28 into Canterbury with the villages of Westmarsh, Ware and East Stourmouth delineating the boggy space.

The marshland itself was laid out like a series of fields, but he'd learned the boundaries were watercourses; drainage ditches that had been cut into the boggy land to draw the water away from the naturally low-lying land and help prevent flooding. The River Stour sliced through the centre of the part of the map Gray was looking at, before joining with what was left of the Wantsum Channel, once a waterway up to a mile wide yet now just a tiny, silted-up gully which meandered down to Canterbury.

A dotted line on the map indicated a path, starting from where they were, although it petered out once the route met with the River Stour. Otherwise paths ran either side of the river, but none seemed to join up; they ran for a distance, then stopped.

"I think we'll just have to see what we find," said Gray. He had nothing better to suggest and neither, it seemed, did Pfeffer or Roza.

IT HAD BEEN RAINING for more than half an hour. Gray learned pretty quickly that his coat wasn't fully waterproof, particularly at the seams where he was now wet. And his jeans were soaked through from pushing through long grass and his feet sinking into boggy ground. He was thoroughly uncomfortable and miserable. Pfeffer and Roza, in comparison, possessed the proper gear and were perfectly happy.

"I don't know," grumbled Gray. "Maybe I was wrong." They'd searched every construction that appeared remotely feasible for Myerscough to use as a hideout. It felt like they'd been trudging for miles. Perhaps Hamson was right and Myerscough had travelled through the area on his way to somewhere else. But where?

Pfeffer poured a cup of tea from a flask. Roza had a cup also. The tea steamed. Gray took a sip. The taste wasn't great, but it was hot.

"Why though, Sol? Why would Myerscough head across the marshland to be collected on the other side? It doesn't make sense." Exactly the argument Gray had delivered to Hamson. Pfeffer shook her head. "No, I think he's here somewhere."

Gray checked the map before handing it to Roza. Nearby a building was marked on the map as a simple block outline. It could be anything. Gray lifted the binoculars hanging around his neck, focused on a structure made of slatted blackened wood, surrounded by a rough paling fence. He could see a door but no windows. "Seems to be an animal shed." There were some sheep on the land; the vegetation here was poor. Hardly top quality agricultural land.

He drained the last of the drink, shook the drops onto the grass and handed the cup back to Pfeffer. "Let's have a look," sighed Gray. She slid the flask into her backpack and shouldered the bag.

Gray led them around a wide flooded area. His foot sank in another boggy section; his socks were sodden anyway but the squealch of water between his toes made him shudder. It took them nearly five minutes to pick their way across the land, no path to follow.

A gate allowed access to the enclosure. Gray rattled the door, but the catch held firm – a rusty padlock hung off the hasp. He came back out of the space, leant against the paling fence with the map in his hand again. "We've checked everything on here that seems remotely like a building."

"Do you want to give up?" asked Pfeffer.

"Maybe," said Gray. "I don't know." He was getting colder, the jeans clinging to his thighs.

Pfeffer pointed. "What about over there?"

Several hundred yards away was a line of tightly packed trees. With his naked eye all Gray could spot was the blur of trunks and branches. "I don't see any buildings."

"And there is nothing on the map." Roza tapped a blank space.

"Try the binoculars," said Pfeffer.

He used them once more. Through the lens was a different picture. "I think you're right, Melanie. There's something behind the trees. Let's take a look. If it's a bust we can loop around and go back to Minster and find a pub. I could do with a drink and drying out."

"Fine by me."

"Me too," said Roza.

The trees turned out to be deliberately planted. They had to be, as the foliage ran in a straight line and ultimately formed a large rectangle with a gap one end, maybe ten feet wide. In the centre was a shepherd's hut. The pale green paint was flaking and faded. At the windows were curtains. A path led up to the steps and ran towards a break in the trees, a table and two chairs out the front. One of the chairs had fallen over and grass grew long between the legs. Beyond was another, much smaller shed. Possibly an outside toilet.

"It's like a holiday home in the middle of nowhere," said Gray.

"Maybe a glamping site?" asked Pfeffer.

"Who'd want to camp out here?"

"I can see the idea of getting away from it all. Some people will pay a lot for that."

"Whatever works, I guess."

As they neared Gray saw movement at one of the windows. A twitch of the curtain and the pale orb of a face. Moments later the figure of a man descended the steps in a rush, a rucksack over his shoulder. He threw a glance at them. Gray recognised him instantly.

Myerscough.

Gray, Pfeffer and Roza broke into a run. "Myerscough, stop!" shouted Gray, but he didn't. "Police!"

Myerscough glanced again, saw the gap was shrinking. He ditched his rucksack. Both Pfeffer and Roza began to pull ahead of Gray. They were younger for sure and, seemingly, fitter. Gray struggled to keep up, his boots full of sludgy water.

When Pfeffer was within a few feet of Myerscough, he put in an extra spurt and pulled away a little, but then suddenly he was flying forward, arms out like a bad dive into a swimming pool. Pfeffer was on him as soon as he struck the ground, Roza moments behind.

When Gray reached them Pfeffer had a knee in Myerscough's back and was yanking one arm around while Roza lay on his bucking legs. Gray bent at the waist and pulled in deep breaths. Myerscough was making a muffled screeching sound, his face planted into the springy turf.

"What kept you, sir?" said Pfeffer as she brought up Myerscough's other wrist and ratcheted handcuffs into place. She and Roza got off Myerscough, Pfeffer rolled him over. The man was soaking wet and muddy, his hair plastered back. Myerscough sat up, spat dirt and grass. Gray squatted opposite him. Myerscough leaned away, like he and Gray were magnets of the same pole, repelling each other.

"Who are you?" asked Myerscough.

Gray showed his warrant card. "DI Gray. This is DC Pfeffer. And Roza Selimi."

"Where's Lowther?"

"Angus Lowther?"

"Yes! Is he here? Does he know about me?"

"Why?"

"Answer me?!"

"He's not here."

Myerscough visibly relaxed. "You can't tell him."

"Mr Myerscough, you were reported missing by your wife. Lowther called me and said you were helping with a case. What's going on?"

Myerscough shook his head. "I'm not saying."

"Get up," said Gray. "You're coming with us."

"Where?"

"Margate station."

"No." Myerscough strained to pull away.

"If you won't talk here, we'll do it there."

"There's no reason to take me in."

"Resisting arrest," said Pfeffer.

"Bullshit," said Myerscough.

"Up." Gray got hold of Myerscough's arm and tried to get him to stand, but Myerscough pushed his weight down and resisted. "Okay." Gray released Myerscough. "I'll call Lowther then."

"Please, don't," said Myerscough.

"You're not giving me any choice." Gray pulled out his mobile and scrolled through the contacts until he reached Lowther's details. "One way or another you're coming with us." Gray tapped the screen before showing the phone to Myerscough. "It's ringing."

Myerscough struggled to his feet. "No!" Gray put the phone to his ear. "All right, I'll talk!" Gray didn't move. "Dammit, man, I'll tell you everything!"

Gray ended the call, said, "Okay."

"There's two conditions."

"You're not really in any position to make demands."

"They're necessary."

"Go on, but if I'm not satisfied I'll ring Lowther again."

Myerscough waited until Gray put his phone away. "Not at the station and you can't tell Sylvia you've found me. It isn't safe for her."

"Why?"

"The Albanians have one of your people on their payroll."

Thirty Three

Gray pressed the lift button and waited for the mechanism to kick into action. Myerscough stood next to him, braced by Pfeffer. Roza stood behind. Myerscough's rucksack was over Gray's shoulder; they'd retrieved it before heading back to Gray's car. Myerscough seemed shrunk into himself, maybe trying to make himself appear as unobtrusive as possible.

For the whole of the journey from Minster to Broadstairs Myerscough had lain down on the rear seat, curled up so he didn't encroach onto Roza. When they'd been passing through Broadstairs itself Myerscough sank into the footwell, not moving until Gray pulled up in the underground car park beneath his flat. Gray wasn't happy to be keeping Myerscough here, but he couldn't think of anywhere else.

Myerscough tensed when the lift doors opened. Gray could feel the man's muscles tighten. When all that was revealed was an empty, brightly lit metal box Myerscough physically relaxed a little. Gray entered first, followed by Myerscough, Pfeffer and Roza. They rode upwards in silence.

Inside Gray's flat Myerscough glanced around. He sighed when Gray closed the door and locked it.

"This'll do," said Myerscough. "I'll need somewhere to get changed. You lot made a bit of a mess of me." Myerscough's fear had gone, replaced by a brash confidence.

"You can have the spare bedroom," said Gray. He pointed to a door the far side of the living space. "There's an en-suite if you want a shower."

"These will have to come off." Myerscough lifted his arms. He rattled the handcuffs like Marley's ghost. "I'm hardly able to get out of my clothes if these are attached to me, now can I?"

Pfeffer looked to Gray. "Go ahead," he said.

While Pfeffer was unlocking the cuffs Myerscough said, "Will you get me a coffee, love? Strong, with two sugars. While I'm getting changed."

"It's not a problem," said Pfeffer before Gray responded. "I could do with something too."

"Good girl," said Myerscough. He walked to the spare room, paused at the door. "I'd appreciate my clothes, inspector." Gray tossed Myerscough the rucksack. Myerscough went into the room, opened the en-suite door and poked his head inside before moving to the window and taking in the view.

He found Pfeffer and Roza in the kitchen. Pfeffer already had the kettle on, placed three mugs and the milk on the kitchen unit and was searching through the cupboards. "Where's your coffee?" she asked. Gray got her the packet. "Thanks."

"How's this going to work?" asked Pfeffer.

"We're four floors up," said Gray. "So I'm pretty sure Myerscough won't be jumping from the bedroom window. I'll sleep on the sofa so he can't get out the front door."

"You'll need help. I'll stay as well."

"I can too, if you like," said Roza.

"Just one of us, I think," said Pfeffer, firmly. "Not enough beds."

"Fine by me."

"There's no need," said Gray.

"It's already decided, Sol," said Pfeffer. The boiling kettle clicked off. "Don't think you're going to stop me."

"Okay." Gray raised his hands in surrender. "You can have my room."

"Sure."

"What are we going to do tomorrow?" she asked. "When we both have to be back in the office. What's to stop Myerscough walking out?"

"I don't know yet."

"While you think on it, I'll go back to my flat and get my stuff. I'll be as quick as I can."

IT WAS ANOTHER QUARTER of an hour before Myerscough emerged from the spare room. He was clean and fresh, his hair neatly brushed. But his shirt and trousers were wrinkled. "I'll need some of my stuff washing," he said. "I've pretty much run out."

"There's a machine," said Gray. He was sitting on the sofa, feeling better now he'd had a shower and changed clothes. "Your coffee was made a while ago." He pointed to the mug on the table next to him.

"I don't mind. I can't drink anything too hot, hurts my oesophagus."

When Myerscough took the first sip of his drink he sighed like a parched man in a desert having his first water for days.

"Where are our friends?" asked Myerscough. "Have they skipped out on us?"

"They've gone. But DC Pfeffer will be back."

"I'd say she has a liking for you." Myerscough winked. "I have a knack for these things."

"We're just colleagues."

"Sure."

"Why were you hiding out in the marshland?"

"Shouldn't you be taping me?"

"We're not having an official discussion, not right now."

"So this is off the record?"

"As much as it can be," said Gray. "I'm still a police officer. However, I think you need somebody's help, and that somebody can be me, but only if I know what's going on. Otherwise I'm guessing."

"Sylvia mentioned you enough times. And not much of it good."

"Nice to hear."

Myerscough drained the mug, put it back on the table. "How is she?"

"Worried about you."

Myerscough pulled a face, like he was in pain. "I didn't want to do this to her, but it's for the best. She's safer this way."

"So you said. Again, why you were out in the marshland?"

"Because I was scared for my life. Couldn't you tell by my reaction when you came for me?"

"People run for lots of different reasons, Mr Myerscough."

"Very true. And call me Jasper, I can't abide formality."

"You mentioned the Albanians have someone on their payroll inside the station. Who?"

"That detail was kept from me. It could be one person, or maybe several. Either way, Krisniqi knows quite a bit about how you lot work. Look, I think we need to go back to the beginning."

"Okay."

"My name actually isn't Jasper Myerscough. Well, it is now, but that's not the name I was born with." Myerscough held up a hand before Gray could speak. "And no, I'm not going to tell you what it originally was. There are some specifics you can't know.

"Some years ago I became involved in a drugs ring where I lived in London. Trouble was I eventually took a lot of my own gear, because of the stress. I became paranoid and dangerous. I was careless and flashed the cash too much. I drove an Aston Martin and lived in a huge house, but my job was a used car sales manager, before that I'd been in logistics. I utilised the cars to move cachets of drugs around.

"Needless to say, I got busted. I was stopped for speeding with a big bag of coke in the glove compartment." Myerscough shook his head. "So stupid. The police threw me in the cells and let me stew for a couple of hours. Eventually a man calling himself Angus Lowther walked in. He told me the cops knew exactly who I was and what I'd been doing. There had been an undercover operation running for some time, monitoring all my activities. It was my flashing the cash which had alerted the cops to me.

"I thought I was done for. I was scared to death of losing my family. Lowther tossed me a lifeline then. He told me that ultimately the police wanted the top layer, I was relatively small fry. If I went down I'd soon be replaced. However, the people running the drugs operation were careful. They had nothing to do with the gear itself. So we made a bargain. I'd be released right away with a caution but I was to help the cops entrap the bosses. Or I'd be sent down. It was an easy choice, I'll tell you. Lowther became my handler."

"What family?"

"I have a wife and two kids. Or had, I should say."

"Where are they?"

"As far as they're concerned, I don't exist anymore." Myerscough paused for a moment. "Anyway, to cut a long and freakish story short, I did manage to gather enough evidence and arrests were made. I appeared in court as a witness, so of course my involvement emerged and I left behind my family for their good. So you see, I've had practice at running."

"And you came to Thanet."

"I was sent. I entered witness protection, got a new name and a few quid to look after myself. It was a big comedown, I tell you. Thanet was the third location they moved me to. I was tired and I stayed put. I met Sylvia and the rest is history."

"Why her?"

"I was poor and lonely. Sylvia was wealthy and lonely. It seemed like a good match. She doesn't ask about my past and she's always pleased to see me when I come home. She's like a faithful dog."

"I'm sure she'd love that description."

Myerscough shrugged. "Whatever, it's true."

"How did you come into contact with the Albanians?"

Myerscough shifted in his seat. "Can I have a drink? Something strong this time. Like a whisky."

Gray poured a large shot, handed the glass over.

Myerscough downed half of the brown liquid, rested the glass on the arm of the seat. "Lowther knocked on my door one day, completely out of the blue. I hadn't seen him for several years. He looked bloody dreadful. Like he'd aged a decade. I panicked, him standing there bold as brass.

"I dragged him down to the local pub so Sylvia wouldn't see him. We weren't married then by the way. Lowther told me he needed my help with something. There was a gang bringing drugs into the UK via the Dover ferry port. He wanted me to use my experience to find out who was running the operation and implicate them. Of course I said no. It was the last thing I wanted to do, get back into that life. I wasn't given any choice. Lowther threatened to reveal my location to the London gang I'd helped put behind bars."

Myerscough drank the rest of the whisky. "The bastard, I could have killed him there and then. He grinned at me like he knew I was done, which I was. Lowther promised me it wouldn't be for long. Just enough to get an arrest. So I reluctantly agreed, moved jobs to Langham's and started digging."

"Did you succeed?" asked Gray.

"Yes and no. There were arrests. Lowther told me a cop in London was pulled in."

"Lewis Strang?"

"Do you know him?"

"I was involved in the case."

"With Strang going down I thought I was free, but Lowther didn't let me off the hook. The supply route was immediately taken over – the suppliers became the distributors."

"The Albanians?"

"Correct. Lowther saw a chance to take down a pan-European structure. You should have seen the light in his eyes when he was talking about it, Sol. He was like a preacher, all spit and fire. Nothing else mattered, including me.

"My role was as an intermediary. I ensured the trucks got in, before handing them over to a cut out. I never worked directly with either gang. But Lowther had told me who the Albanians were, showed me some pictures and shared names."

"Any in particular?"

"Krisniqi was the main one. The day he came into Langham's." Myerscough shook his head. "I froze when I saw him standing in reception. He caught sight of me and winked. He clearly knew who I was, where I worked. I couldn't believe it. I backed up, rang Lowther straight away. I wanted out, of course. Lowther wasn't interested. He'd become more and more unstable, I just couldn't trust him. It was hard to believe his management were allowing Lowther to continue operating. There was nobody I could rely on and I wanted to keep Sylvia safe so I upped and cleared off to the marshland."

"You left Sylvia alone and vulnerable. That's hardly protecting her."

Myerscough rubbed his face. "I wasn't thinking at the time. Once I'd left i wasn't sure what to do to return. And feeling free of Lowther was incredible."

"I was told recently that drug supply into Kent has been interrupted because a key person had gone missing. I assume that's you."

"I'm the linchpin." Myerscough rubbed his eyes. "By the way, Langham knows nothing about what's being done with his trucks. He's a good man and entirely innocent."

"You'll excuse me if I don't take you at your word."

"God, what a mess. I could really do with some sleep. I've barely slept a wink for days."

"I've more questions for you."

"They'll have to wait, I'm done." Myerscough stood. "Thanks for the whisky."

As Myerscough was closing the bedroom door the entrance buzzer sounded. It was Pfeffer. She was carrying a gym bag in one hand and had changed into a tracksuit. "Where is he?" she asked, handing back Gray's car keys.

"Gone to get some sleep, but we spoke. Stick your bag in the bedroom and I'll tell you all about it."

When she was back and seated where Myerscough had been he repeated his conversation with the man, his voice low so it didn't carry.

"We still don't have all the answers," said Pfeffer when Gray finished.

"Not by a long stretch."

"I'm hungry," said Pfeffer.

"I haven't got much in."

"How about a takeaway curry?"

"I can get one delivered."

Gray ordered the food, then unscrewed the cap on a bottle of Merlot and poured Pfeffer a glass. "I've had a thought about tomorrow," said Gray. "I'm owed some lieu time, I'll take the day off."

"And after?"

"I'll figure that out when I get there."

"Are you going to tell DCI Hamson what he said? About us having someone on the Albanian's payroll?"

"He could be lying."

"And he could be telling the truth. What if it's Hamson herself?"

Gray had been considering that. "I don't believe so."

"Do you know for sure?"

"No," said Gray. How could he?

"Equally, it might be me."

"Possibly, Melanie, but not so likely." Pfeffer was new to the police, with few connections. "If I had any doubts then I wouldn't have brought you along."

"Who then?"

"I wish I knew."

"There's Roza," said Pfeffer.

"It can't be. Myerscough said somebody in the station."

"And where's she working?"

Odell House. He said, "She's only just arrived."

"I've no idea then," said Pfeffer. "But I can tell you one thing for free. I don't trust her."

SOMETHING DRAGGED GRAY from his sleep. A noise. In the dimness someone moved around. Too small to be Myerscough, so it must be Pfeffer. She headed into the kitchen. He heard a tap run. Getting herself a drink. A few moments later she leant against the door jamb, facing him. He didn't move. What was she thinking?

Then Pfeffer pushed off, tiptoed slowly over. Gray closed his eyes, leaving just a slit open. She paused a few feet away. She was wearing a t-shirt, exposing her legs and arms. And a pair of white knickers. Gray didn't move a muscle, breathed steadily so it seemed like he was asleep. Pfeffer stood there, just watching him. Eventually she turned, went back to her bedroom as silently as she'd come and closed the door.

Gray rolled over. What the hell that had been all about?

Thirty Four

Pfeffer woke Gray the following morning, attempting to creep out of the flat. She was at the door, twisting the key in the lock. "Sorry," she said. "I was trying not to disturb you."

"No problem," said Gray, rubbing his eyes. "What time is it?" There was a low light pushing through the curtains.

"Just after 6.30."

"Do you want the car keys?"

"I'm going to jog in."

Gray sat up. "Are you mad?"

"It's only four and a half miles." She hefted a small backpack. "I'll get a shower and changed at the other end. I do it every day." No wonder Pfeffer had been able to chase down Myerscough yesterday. "I'll see you this evening. I'll bring pizza." And then she was gone.

Gray stuck the kettle on and grabbed a fast shower. When he came out Myerscough was pouring hot water onto a tea bag.

"How did you sleep?" asked Gray.

"Hardly at all." Myerscough got milk from the fridge. "I've made a decision. I'm done with all of this, with Lowther. I've served my debt. I just want to go home to Sylvia, live a quiet life."

Gray leant against the counter. "Shouldn't you be telling Lowther that?"

"He won't listen. All he cares about is his job, not the consequences. So, I have a proposal. I've been in touch with my contacts in Eastern Europe and I know when the next shipment's coming in. Krisniqi is desperate to get hold of some gear. If he doesn't fulfil his buyer's needs, somebody else will. Simple economics, right?"

"And?"

"I can tell you where to be. You sweep up the drugs, Krisniqi, his gang, the lot in one fell swoop. I'll be free and you're the hero."

The opportunity to put such a major dent in the local drug supply was a powerful one. "When is it arriving?" asked Gray.

"Tomorrow morning, very early."

"Not long to plan."

"Then you'll need with speak with your boss. Don't worry about leaving me here. I'm not going anywhere. If Krisniqi gets wind of my location I'm a dead man."

"The thought had never crossed my mind."

"WHAT HAPPENED TO TAKING a day's holiday?" asked Hamson when Gray walked into her office less than an hour later. She was seated at her desk, fingers paused over her laptop.

"I found Myerscough," said Gray. "In the Minster marshlands, where I thought he'd be."

"Well done, I'm sure Sylvia will be pleased."

"He doesn't want to see her." Hamson shifted away from her laptop, gave Gray her full attention.

"Why?"

"He's been acting as a distributor for drugs shipments, bringing in heroin, coke and meth via Dover using Langham's lorries, that's the place where he works."

"And he told you all this outright?"

"He's been working undercover on behalf of the NCA. Angus Lowther is his handler. The guy who called me a couple of days ago. Lowther was pretty keen to find Myerscough. I understand why now."

"I remember. I assume you've called Lowther and let him know?"

"Myerscough says he was coerced into the role he's playing now. He's got previous for handling drugs. He was caught, worked for Lowther, turned state evidence and entered the witness protection programme. Until Lowther needed him again. That's where the coercion comes in."

"Jesus."

"That's not all. The Albanians know about Myerscough too. It was him running which put the squeeze on supply. There's a truck coming in first thing tomorrow, loaded with drugs. Myerscough reckons he can hand it to us. We can sweep up most if not all of the gang there and then."

"How many people are we talking about?"

"Maybe six."

"Maybe?"

"Myerscough said he's never been to a handover so he's not totally sure."

"Where's it going down?"

"Myerscough is keeping that information to himself for now as a bargaining chip."

"Great."

"We could make a big impact, Von."

"So you've said, but it doesn't sound like our kind of op. Perhaps the NCA should be handling this."

"There isn't the time. In under twenty four hours there's a whole heap of narcotics arriving on our patch."

"Then we should notify Border Control. They can stop the truck."

"But all that'll happen is we get the driver and the drugs."

"Which is pretty good."

"And a drop in the ocean. If we do as Myerscough suggests then we catch a lot of them and probably get more evidence that leads to further convictions."

"You don't know that for sure, Sol."

"Right, but at least we have a chance! We've been on the back foot for months. Even Pivot wasn't really the success we thought it would be. We can do something significant here, if we just take the opportunity."

Hamson regarded Gray for a long moment. "Okay," she said eventually. "What you're suggesting has merit. But there's two caveats. The first is we plan this as thoroughly as we can in the time available."

"Of course."

"And the other is I want to speak with Myerscough myself." Hamson stood.

"Myerscough isn't in the cells. You'll have to come to my flat."

"Why not?"

"That's the other complication, Myerscough claims the Albanians have someone in the station on their payroll."

"Who?"

"He has no idea."

Thirty Five

Myerscough was sitting on the balcony when Gray and Hamson entered the flat. He was facing out to sea, cup in hand.

"DCI Yvonne Hamson," she said.

"Pleased to meet you," said Myerscough. "I wish it were under better circumstances. I heard a lot about you from Sylvia. She liked you."

"Nice to hear, Mr Myerscough, but this isn't a popularity contest. Maybe we should go back inside and talk privately."

Once in the living room and the French windows closed Hamson continued, "DI Gray has explained your situation and proposal but I have further questions before I agree to go ahead."

Myerscough grinned. "I suspected you might."

"I'd like to know where the delivery is going to be made."

"One of the warehouses on Manston airport."

"Makes sense, a large space where nobody goes now it's closed down," said Gray.

"How does the process work?" asked Hamson.

"I have people at the port who select which vehicles to check, far too many come in to do every one, mine get waved through, but just in case of a cursory search the palett is tucked back a little. Takes longer to unload, though lessens the chance of casual discovery.

"The lorry arrives at the warehouse. There's a fork lift waiting and a handful of men. The truck is in and out within ten minutes so it appears on the tachometer as if the driver took a toilet break. Once the truck has gone then the palett gets broken down. The drugs are already packaged into one kilo bags. The shipment is split and placed into cars and driven off to be cut and distributed out to the needy population."

"You make it sound like a public service," said Hamson.

"Sorry, just my little joke."

"So, the only time all the drugs are in one place are either on the truck or in the warehouse at the point of delivery?" asked Gray.

"Correct," said Myerscough. "But in the warehouse is the optimum time. That's when everybody's present."

"Okay," said Hamson. "I'd like to see where it's going to happen and you're going show me, Mr Myerscough."

"I could be seen."

"Wear a hat and glasses then."

"HERE," SAID MYERSCOUGH, pointing. He was hunched over on the back seat where he'd been laid the whole trip.

Gray slowed as he neared a set of large metal gates, easily ten feet high, set into the perimeter chainlink fence which ran around the expanse which was Manston airport, once the second longest runway in England and an ex-WWII base. Now it was disused, the concrete runway being split by weeds, the buildings beginning to decay, while the owners and council argued over its future. A large padlocked chain looped through the gates.

"Keep going!" said Myerscough.

But Gray ignored Myerscough, craning his neck to stare through the fence. Hamson, beside him in the passenger seat, doing the same. Beyond stood a hangar, once used for a helicopter maintenance business, and a pair of block buildings constructed from cast concrete. The doors to both were closed.

"This was the cold storage unit," said Gray. "I used to see lorries in and out of here all the time. What time are they due?"

"Around 5am. I can't be more exact. Sometimes there are delays to the crossing."

"It's a good location," said Hamson. "Very few houses nearby and none which overlook the entrance."

"And Manston Road is often used by cars and trucks as a shortcut to the A299 just up the road so nobody would think it odd to see lorries along here."

"But going in and out of the airport?"

"I bet hardly anyone will notice."

"I think we've seen enough," said Hamson. "Let's head back to yours and start planning. There's a lot to do before tonight."

Gray pressed the accelerator. "So, that's a yes?"

"Don't make me regret it." That phrase again.

"You won't." Gray hoped he was right.

GRAY RUBBED HIS EYES. He was tired. But so were the others. They'd reconvened at his flat late afternoon – Hamson, Pfeffer and Gray. Then, with Myerscough providing detail when requested, the three cops had kicked around several possible scenarios as to how the operation might unfold over the following hours. Hamson drove the conversation, Pfeffer took notes. Myerscough sat back slightly from the discussion, not happy as he'd been told he was joining the raid.

"We have to keep this small," said Hamson, repeating herself.

"How?" asked Gray. He picked up a spring roll and bit into it. Another takeaway, Chinese, not pizza. The spring roll was cold, the meaty contents congealed and sticky. "We'll need most of our uniforms on this to surround the gang and sweep everyone up. There's no way this is going to be a tight operation."

"What about the mole?"

"I've been thinking about that. I reckon I might know who it is. Roza."

"You brought her in, Sol. That's great, well done."

"It was Melanie's idea."

"Don't go blaming Melanie. I distinctly remember you telling me she was joining the team temporarily."

Gray held his hands up. "No, I mean it was her who suggested Roza might be the mole."

"The Albanians have only been in Thanet a few months, right? Is that long enough to draw in a police officer and be paying them for information?"

"I've no idea," said Gray "You'd have to ask an expert like Yarrow."

"Roza has family back in her country. Maybe they've been put under pressure. And they killed her brother."

"So she says, Von. Do we have any proof? How could we possibly check? And she's managed to come up with the identity of several of the gang rather quickly. Information that's proved largely useless to us. They're just names." Gray let Hamson think on his theories for a few moments. "I'm right, Von. I know I am."

Hamson rubbed the bridge of her nose. "Okay, I haven't got any better suggestions."

"I'll ring Emily, ask her to have a chat with Yarrow about Roza's background."

"All right. Until we know more keep Roza away from the operation."

"Understood."

Hamson stood. "Anyway, I think we're done. I've cancelled all leave so we've got the maximum number of bodies available. I'll see you at the station at 4.00am for the briefing. Get some rest, if you can."

When Hamson had left Gray started clearing up the detritus from the takeaway.

"I still don't see why I have to be there," said Myersough, not bothering to help.

"We've been over this," said Gray. "You're essential. Without you we don't know what we're looking for."

"It could be dangerous."

"You'll be safe. Melanie will stay with you on the fringes."

Myerscough pursed his lips. "I suppose I don't have much choice."

"Not really."

"I'm off to sleep." Myerscough went into the bedroom, closed the door, leaving Pfeffer and Gray alone.

"Do you want to do the same?" asked Gray.

"What, are you asking me to go to bed?" asked Pfeffer. Her eyes were wide, like Gray had made some terrible suggestion.

"No, I didn't mean that!"

Pfeffer laughed. "I was joking. You should see your face!"

"Sorry."

"Why, would it be that bad if we did?"

"I'm in a relationship, Melanie."

"So? It's called friends with benefits."

"You're still joking, right?" Gray wasn't sure what the hell was going on.

"If you want. Why don't we take a drink out on the balcony?"

"Coffee?"

"Only if you're interested in staying awake, otherwise I'll have something a bit stronger."

"I've got gin." Hamson had bought him a bottle for Christmas. It remained unopened in the cabinet.

"Sure."

Gray poured two glasses out. He had some tonic which still retained its fizz. He took the drinks onto the balcony where Pfeffer sat. She'd got the table top gas burner going and it was throwing out a reasonable heat. "Here you are," said Gray, handing over the G&T. "Just the one before the operation."

"Spoilsport," said Pfeffer. "To tomorrow." She clinked Gray's glass. He sat beside her and looked out to sea. "If the general population at the station was aware I'm staying here with you right now, it'd be scandal left, right and centre."

"What I told you earlier, about being in a relationship. I'd appreciate you keeping it quiet because nobody else knows, okay?"

"I assume DCI Hamson is the lucky girl?"

"She's not. But my girlfriend is in the police."

"Girlfriend?" Pfeffer laughed. "Sounds like the sort of thing you say when you're a teenager."

"What other word should I use. Partner?"

"I'm not the best person to ask." Pfeffer shrugged. "Why do you keep it quiet?"

"I'm not keen on people talking about me. The less I share, the less there is to say."

"You're good at keeping secrets, then."

Gray snorted. "I guess so."

Pfeffer drained her drink then held up the glass. "I'm all out of gin."

They stayed on the balcony for another hour, chatting. Eventually, Gray said, "No jokes this time, but I need some sleep."

Pfeffer held her hand up. "Fine with me."

After brushing his teeth Gray threw a blanket over the sofa cushions, turned off the lights and lay down. Despite what he'd said to Pfeffer, he wasn't tired. He stared at the ceiling for a few minutes, thinking about the operation. Then he heard light footsteps and Pfeffer squatted down beside him.

"What's the matter?" asked Gray.

"Absolutely nothing," whispered Pfeffer and kissed him before she stood and removed her t-shirt. Then she slid under the blanket on top of him.

Thirty Six

5.30am.

The drugs delivery was overdue. Gray was parked on a nearby road out of sight of the gate in an unmarked car, Hamson in the passenger seat, Myerscough and Pfeffer in the rear. Nearby were three vans, loaded with uniformed officers awaiting the signal to go in.

A second unmarked vehicle sat behind Gray's – for Pfeffer and Myerscough during the operation. Pfeffer had expressed her frustration to Gray about having to babysit Myerscough. Nothing, though, had been said by either of them about what happened last night and that was bothering Gray.

"Lorry approaching." A male voice over the radio, a uniform who had been stationed on the approach road. There was only one way in and one way out so monitoring was straightforward.

Gray twisted in his seat. "Time for you guys to leave." Without a word Myerscough and Pfeffer popped their doors. Gray followed. "Melanie, one second."

"Sir?"

He waited while Myerscough got into the second vehicle. "About last night."

"There's nothing to say."

"But we..."

"Sir, this isn't the time or place." Pfeffer walked away, joined Myerscough. She was right. Gray returned to his car.

"There," said Hamson and pointed. Both completely unnecessary as the Langham's livery on the truck's side was obvious as it passed slowly by. Gray caught the flare of brake lights and the truck lost even more speed. The driver didn't bother to indicate before the cab swung left, followed by the trailer.

The truck went straight on, heading for the hangar. As the vehicle approached, the huge double doors slid back. They were so large they had to be mechanised. The truck paused until it could move inside then the doors began to shut. Gray turned on the engine.

Hamson got on the radio. "Go, go."

Gray hit the accelerator and they bumped onto Manston Road. Within moments they were on the hangar approach road along with the three vans. Two of the vans peeled off, one heading for the hangar door while the other aimed for the far side of the building. Floor plans revealed there were two additional side entrances.

Gray pulled up next to the hangar wall, the remaining van just behind. The van's rear doors burst open and ten uniformed officers spilled out, Worthington among them. Two men were carrying a metal battering ram called Bessie, which Gray knew from experience was heavy and cumbersome, but very effective. The team ran towards the nearby door.

Hamson's radio squelched. "In place," said a voice. Hamson nodded.

Bessie was swung back, then forth. A huge crash as metal struck wood. The door splintered, but didn't give way. Three more blows and the jamb broke. Uniform spilled in, briefly slowed by having to squeeze through the narrow entrance. Hamson and Gray brought up the rear.

The interior was a huge, open space. A high ceiling with bright, conical spotlights, each a couple of feet in diameter, hung at regular interviews, bathing the concrete floor in a harsh light. The truck sat in the centre of the open area, the rear doors were open and a man sat in a fork lift truck.

"Police, police! Nobody move!" shouted Hamson.

Suddenly, the three men burst into motion. They ran for the exit on the opposite side of the hangar but then checked as uniform spilled in from there as well. The three men split up, heading in different directions. However, there was nowhere to go and quickly the trio were rounded up and marched back towards Gray and Hamson. Gray didn't recognise any of the men.

"Split them up," said Hamson. So they couldn't speak to each other and agree a story. She turned to Gray. "Myerscough said there would likely be six or so here. Where are the rest?"

"I don't know."

Gray moved to the truck. He was faced with brown cardboard boxes, piled onto wooden pallets, each pile wrapped with clear plastic film to hold the structure steady and protect the packaging from dirt and water.

"Let's see what we've got," said Hamson and clambered up into the rear. Gray pulled himself up too. He tore at the plastic film to reach the top of the boxes which were taped down. When he opened them he found folded textiles.

"Clothes," said Gray.

"Likewise," said Hamson.

Gray couldn't reach any further because the boxes were tightly packed. He dropped down onto the floor. "Which of you was going to unload?"

"Me." A dark haired man, pockmarked face, Welsh accent. Gray could smell the body odour.

"I want you to get down some of the pallets."

"I can't."

"Why?"

"One of your men hurt my arm when they grabbed me. I'm unable to operate the levers on the forklift."

Gray didn't believe him, but neither could he force the driver to comply.

"I will." Worthington stepped forward. "I used to work in a warehouse before joining up."

"Go ahead," said Gray.

Worthington swung himself onto the fork lift before dropping into the seat. He certainly seemed to be familiar with the controls. Worthington twisted the key and the engine roared into life. A cloud of dark, black smoke billowed from the exhaust behind the cab.

He backed up before swinging towards the truck, lifting the forks up at the same time and sliding the forks dextrously under a pallet. He reversed and deposited the load a few yards away. Hamson raised an eyebrow.

"Keep going," shouted Gray over the engine.

When Worthington had four pallets down Gray raised his hand. Worthington killed the engine and only then did Gray realise quite how loud it had been.

Worthington jumped down, a big grin on his face. "Like old times!"

"Let's get looking," said Gray.

Four of the uniform started unloading the boxes from the pallet and opening them. Gray got back inside the truck and opened more, but all they found were more textiles.

"Anything?" asked Hamson.

"Not yet." Gray turned to Worthington. "Pull off another row of pallets would you?"

Worthington fired up the truck again and got to work. With the second pallet removed, Gray saw something was different. A pile of white boxes in the middle of the brown ones. The fork lift's engine died once more. Gray opened the white box, found packets and packets of cigarettes, a brand he didn't recognise. He showed them to Hamson.

"Where are the drugs?" she asked.

"Whoa, whoa," said the driver. "What drugs? I don't know what you're talking about."

"We had intelligence that this was a drugs run," said Gray.

"Bloody hell, no. Just fags, mate. Sometimes booze. Never drugs!"

"Right," said Hamson. "Get these three down the station."

The men were arrested for smuggling, read their rights and led away.

"Bring Myerscough in," said Hamson, once the three were in the back of a van and being driven off. "Let's see what he has to say about this, because nothing is making any sense."

Gray pulled out his mobile and dialled Pfeffer's number. After a few rings it dropped into voicemail. He tried again, got the same result. Gray nodded at one of the uniform. "Can you get on your radio and contact DC Pfeffer, please."

The uniform pressed the button on his Airwave. "DC Pfeffer, come in. DC Pfeffer, over." He tried several times but got no answer.

"What the hell is going on?" asked Hamson, but Gray was already running. Outside he leapt into his car, started the engine and made a wide one hundred and eighty degree turn. He raced along the service road, back onto Manston Road then across to where Pfeffer was parked. He slewed to a halt a few feet away. Both passenger and driver door were wide open.

Gray dashed round the rear of the car and almost fell over something on the ground. It was Pfeffer, lying on her side, curled into the foetal position. Gray hunted for a pulse, felt a flutter under his fingertips.

He got onto the radio. "Officer down, request ambulance to Manston Road immediately."

Gray returned to Pfeffer, waiting the arrival of help and willed her to be all right. But he couldn't see Myerscough. Where the hell was he? And what had he done to Pfeffer?

Thirty Seven

"What a clusterfuck," said Hamson. She was seated behind her desk, Gray at her conference table, nursing a coffee. "The superintendent has already chewed my arse off and he's coming back for another bite shortly, once he's reported up through his structure. I fully expect any crap flowing downhill is going to land squarely on me. I wish I'd just handed the op over to the NCA."

Gray didn't reply. He was shattered but couldn't possibly sleep.

"How is Pfeffer?" asked Hamson.

"Hanging in. Once she wakes, I'll speak with her to find out what I can."

An ambulance had arrived within minutes and whisked Pfeffer off to the hospital. She'd been badly beaten. She remained unconscious and in a stable condition. The area surrounding Pfeffer's car was now a crime scene, with CSI crawling all over it.

"Jesus, this couldn't have gone any bloody worse." Hamson rubbed the bridge of her nose. "One of our own battered to within a whisker of her life and a witness disappeared. All for a measly haul of contraband cigarettes."

"None of the men we arrested knew anything. Two are locals. The driver is from Cardiff. He picks up cigarettes or booze whenever he's over on the continent, hands a few over to the border guards if he's stopped, then drives to Thanet. Apparently, this isn't the first time they've unloaded at Manston. It seems to be a regular operation," said Gray. "The only coincidence is the truck being owned by Langham."

"No association with Krisniqi or his gang?"

"Not that we can find yet."

"Maybe Myerscough got his timings wrong."

"He lied to us, Von. Myerscough must have surprised Pfeffer and run, it's the only explanation."

"It makes no sense." Hamson's phone rang. "Marsh," she said with a heavy sigh. "Wish me luck."

As Gray left her office his own mobile vibrated. "Hi Emily," he said. He felt a slice of guilt after his liaison with Pfeffer last night.

"I've just heard, are you all right?" she said.

"I'm fine, but one of my colleagues is in a bad way."

"Yarrow told me, Hamson's been on the phone to him, but he didn't get all the details. What happened?"

"I wish I knew for sure." Gray leant against the wall, hung his head. "This is bad, really bad. Thanks for calling, by the way, I appreciate it."

"It's not just that, you asked me about Roza. I talked to Yarrow about her, on the quiet, of course."

"What did you learn?"

"He thinks highly of her."

Gray knew that already. "Did you share my theory with him? That she could be a leak to the Albanians."

"I did, and Yarrow wasn't convinced. He reckons she's not the type to be bribed. They killed her brother, remember."

"Okay."

"I hope that helps?"

"Maybe, I don't know. Look, there's loads going on, I'd better go."

"See you soon."

Gray disconnected.

PFEFFER WAS IN A PRIVATE room just off the main ward at the QEQM hospital. A uniformed officer stationed outside opened the door for Gray.

Pfeffer was propped up in bed, white sheets pulled up to her chest. The light was dim, the curtains closed, a low wattage lamp above her head threw out a little illumination. A drip was connected to her arm. The repetitive bleep from a heart monitor accompanied the in / out breathing of a ventilator.

Gray drew up a chair and perched on the edge. Pfeffer's face was badly bruised, one eye black and closed. The ventilator mask covered her mouth and nose. He didn't know what to do with himself, powerless to change anything.

The door opened and a man in a white lab coat entered. "Oh, sorry, I didn't know you were here. I'm Dr Herbertson."

Gray stood. "DI Gray, Melanie works for me. How is she?"

"Stable is the best I can say. Miss Pfeffer took a good beating, particularly around her abdomen and head. I suspect she was kicked while on the ground. From the marks.On her arms and legs she curled up to protect herself."

"Will she recover fully?"

"At this stage it's hard to say. We've carried out a brain scan and there's some damage, like you'd see on a boxer after a fight.

Frankly, we won't know for sure until she's awake and I can properly assess her."

Gray handed over his business card which Herbertson took. "Would you mind giving me a call if she comes round?"

"Let's be positive and say when, inspector."

As Gray got into the car park his mobile rang. It was Hamson. "How's Pfeffer?"

"Not good. Possible brain damage."

"Bloody hell." She paused briefly. "I've more bad news. A body has been found. It's Myerscough."

Thirty Eight

The Ramsgate Hoverport had been closed for over thirty years. Once it was a hive of activity as hovercraft noisily shuttled between the terminal on Cliffsend across the English Channel to France and back.

Over time lorry freight had become more important and the inability of hovercraft to transport trucks meant the port became unsustainable. Since shutting down decay had set in and nature took back what it lost, very much like the nearby Manston airport – the airfield perimeter fence was about visible from here.

The turning Gray wanted just off the Sandwich Road wasn't obvious, simply a dip on the pavement next to some trees and bushes. Gray knew it anyway, but the presence of a police car and two uniformed officers was a useful guide. They let him through and he drove down a shallow incline.

At the bottom a large, flat space opened up to where there had been buildings, now long gone, and the launch area for the craft to slide off into the brown waters of Pegwell Bay. At low tide the waters receded a mile or so and only the hovercraft had been capable of navigating the mud flats.

Gray parked behind two white CSI vans. The immediate expanse in front was cordoned off. He found the overweight moustachioed Crime Scene Manager, Brian Blake, who logged

Gray's attendance and handed over an evidence suit. Gray shrugged the all-in-one piece over his clothes.

"Follow your nose," said Blake, indicating with his pen for extra emphasis. Gray ducked under the cordon, a strip of police tape which flapped in the sea breeze, and headed for the locus.

Being adjacent to a nature reserve and on a coastal path, walkers sometimes came this route, but up here was off the beaten track; people tended to stay lower down on the beach itself.

Worthington, the Senior Investigating Officer, nodded at Gray as he approached. Next to him stood the pathologist, Clough.

There was the corpse, lying on its front, face turned away from Gray. One arm twisted behind the back in an unnatural angle, both legs straight. A pool of blood surrounded the torso, absorbed by the cracked tarmac and turned a deep maroon colour.

"His throat was cut," said Clough. "By the length and angle of the incision I'd say the stroke occurred while the victim was on the ground. The murderer probably had hold of his hair and cut from left to right, making the assailant righthanded. The cut was deep enough to sever the windpipe. He'd have died quickly."

"Nice," said Gray.

"But he was subjected to a fairly lengthy torture first." Clough pointed to Myerscough's arm. "At least one limb is broken. And I found some cigarette burns and several cut marks on the face, I expect from the same blade which delivered the final stroke. I wouldn't be surprised if I discover more injuries once I get him on a table. Fractures and the like."

Gray walked round the corpse to get a better look. Myerscough's eyes and mouth were wide open. It struck him then. Only a couple of hours ago he'd been speaking to this man and now he was a shell. "Poor bastard."

"I doubt the dogwalker who found Myerscough will forget quickly," said Worthington.

"Time of death?" asked Gray.

"Hard to be accurate, of course," said Clough. Worthington rolled his eyes. "A couple of hours, maybe."

Which would be around the time of the raid. The journey from Manston would only have taken a few minutes. Down here in the early morning light, beneath the level of Sandwich Road and not overlooked, Myerscough had been tortured, then murdered.

"Any CCTV nearby?" asked Gray.

"We're on it," replied Worthington in a tone which conveyed Gray had posed an obvious question, "but I'm not hopeful. All the cameras are on the new road."

"How's DC Pfeffer?" asked Clough.

"Still unconscious," said Gray.

"She's a tough bitch that one," said Worthington.

"Really?" said Clough before Gray could.

Worthington shrugged. "Who's going to inform the next of kin?"

Sylvia.

"I will," said Gray.

Thirty Nine

Gray pulled up outside Sylvia's house in Minnis Bay. She opened the door, waited for him to get out of his car before saying, "What is it, Solomon? Do you have news?"

"Let's talk inside, Sylvia."

She moved out of his way, closed the door, stood in the hallway. "Please, tell me."

"I think you should sit down first."

Sylvia crossed her arms. "I want to know."

"I'm sorry, Sylvia, Jasper's body was found earlier this morning."

"Body? He's dead?"

"I'm sorry," repeated Gray.

"He can't be." Sylvia stared at him. Her expression altered from disbelief to shock as she realised the truth. "Oh my God." She sat down on the stairs, put her head in her hands. "How? How did he die?"

Gray paused. He'd carried out death knocks before. They never got easier, even with experience.

"I expect it'll be on the news soon. You could have reporters coming around to your house. Have you got somewhere else you can stay?"

"I don't give a shit about reporters, Solomon! What the hell happened to him?"

"We're still gathering all the facts."

"Spare me your standard lines. I know how it works."

"He was murdered."

Tears flowed down her cheeks. Then she said, "I think I need a drink now." She went into the living room, poured herself a large measure of vodka from a bottle, sank half of it and topped the glass up.

"How did he die?"

"It's not pleasant," said Gray.

"As you said, I'll find out soon enough."

She was right. "Somebody beat him. And then cut his throat."

Sylvia dropped the drink, the contents splashing across her feet and the carpet. Gray made to pick up the glass. "Leave it," she said. "The stupid, stupid man."

"That's not all, Sylvia." He had to tell her. "Myerscough wasn't his real name."

"What?"

"He once lived in London, was married and ran a car showroom. He was transporting drugs, got arrested and agreed to work with the authorities. But he had to enter the witness protection scheme and changed his identity."

"How long have you known this?"

"A couple of days."

"Why didn't you tell me sooner?"

"I hoped he'd do so himself."

"Who was he then?"

"I don't have that information, I'm afraid."

"You're lying."

"I'm really sorry, Sylvia, but I'm not."

"I don't even know my own husband."

"Is there anything I can do for you?"

"Like what? Bring him back to life?" asked Sylvia. Gray didn't have an answer for that. "Just go, leave me alone."

"Please consider staying elsewhere for the time being. It'll be easier."

"For who, Solomon?" She flopped down into a chair. He heard her sobbing as he let himself out.

Forty

Gray sat in his flat, drinking. Earlier, Hamson had told him Marsh was likely to call for an investigation into the drugs bust that never was. A really crap end to a really crap day.

His mobile rang faintly. He couldn't remember where he'd left it. He followed the sound to the kitchen.

The call dropped as Gray picked up the handset. He entered the contacts list, checked the number. It was local. He called it back and was picked up after a few rings.

"Hello?" A woman's voice that sounded familiar but he couldn't place.

"You just called my number," said Gray.

"It's E, Inspector Gray."

Petrela. "What do you want?"

"You said I was to call if I had anything for you. Well, I do. There's another shipment due."

"When?"

"I want something first."

"Go on."

"My cousin."

Petrela explained exactly what she meant.

"PULL OVER HERE," SAID Gray. The uniform driving the van did so, bumping the vehicle up the kerb. He left the engine running, but killed the headlights. It was late, or early, depending on your perspective. Well after midnight, anyway.

Gray checked the name on the sign – Swinford Gardens, a relatively high-density new-build estate in Cliftonville. This was it. He got out, walked along the road to the cul de sac where the road ended. The terraced house he wanted was opposite, behind a broken wooden fence. One light on upstairs, the curtains were closed, another downstairs. Gray tried the gate. It swung easily.

He returned the way he'd come, opened the rear van doors and climbed in. There were six officers inside. He stood either side of the battering ram lying in the middle of the floor, stooped because of the low roof.

"I want two of you round the back of the house, covering the rear exit. The rest of us go in the front after Bessie has broken down the door." He indicated the battering ram. "My main interest is the girls. If we sweep up some of the punters, that's a bonus, but I want all the women safely in our charge, okay?" He received nods in return. "No messing around, in hard and fast."

Gray got out of the back and into the passenger seat up front. "Let's go."

The driver set off, still with the headlamps unlit, turned into Swinford Gardens and rolled the few hundred yards slowly in first gear before pulling up once more and switching off the engine.

Gray let the officers out of the back. They moved as silently as they could. Gray headed through the gate, pointed to two officers, then along the side of the house. The pair went. Gray counted to twenty before motioning for the ram to be brought to bear. The two officers holding Bessie swung the ram back and forward, building up kinetic energy, crashing the blunt metal instrument into the door with as much force as possible. The door splintered. Gray heard shouts from inside. The officers swung again and this time the door gave way.

Gray stepped over the wreckage, shouting, "Police!" He ran from the hallway into the nearest room, a kitchen where two men had been drinking and playing cards. They were standing, surprise on their faces. A whisky bottle knocked over, its contents running away, soaking into the cash on the table.

One man, wearing a dirty white vest and shorts, bolted for the rear door, but found his way barred by a uniform. He and his fellow gambler were quickly arrested. Gray returned to the hall. Already his colleagues were spreading through the house like antibodies clearing up an infection. He took the steps two at a time, paused briefly at the top. Four doors off the landing, all open. One was a bathroom, the light off, but the interior obvious.

Shouts from further along the corridor. A scream and the smashing of glass. Gray went past two bedrooms, glanced inside. They had similar perspectives, frozen like a photograph – a woman in bed, a naked man standing nearby trying to cover himself up as an officer dealt with the situation.

Gray entered the room at the end. The light was off but enough illumination spilled in from the landing to reveal a shape on the floor. Gray found the switch; a weak beam came from overhead. It was one of his men, flat out, unconscious. Another woman in bed, the sheets pulled up to her neck, gripped tightly between her fingers, clearly terrified. The window was broken. That was what he'd heard.

Looking out, Gray caught sight of a naked man dashing down the street, clothes in his hand. The man glanced back over his shoulder. Krisniqi. Then he was around the corner and gone. Down in the garden another of his men sat on the ground, holding his head in his hands.

"Are you all right?" asked Gray.

The officer stood, unsteady on his feet. "I'm fine. Sorry, sir, he landed on me. I couldn't do anything about it."

Gray turned back to the woman. She had streaky blonde hair, black roots showing through, prominent cheekbones and a black eye.

"I'm police," said Gray, holding up his warrant card. "Everything is going to be fine." The woman pushed herself away from him as far as she could. "Can you show me your ankle please?"

"Why?" she asked.

"Your cousin E sent me."

"E?" asked Agnesca, clearly confused.

"She said you have a tattoo." Agnesca poked a thin leg out from the sheets. There was a fleur de lys in blue ink, just as Petrela had said there would be. "You're safe now."

Forty One

Petrela was waiting for Gray as arranged, in the darkened car park beneath the high rise of Arlington House. Most of the bulbs in the overhead lights were broken. The smell of urine and vomit pervaded the confined space. Gray stopped a few feet away. He felt like a Cold War spy, meeting in the shadows. "It's done. Your cousin is out of the house."

"Where is she?" asked Petrela, emerging from the shadows. "Is she safe?"

"Agnesca is with social services right now. They're taking her to the hospital to get properly checked out."

"Thank you."

"I held up my end of the bargain."

"You did and I made you a promise," said Petrela. "The lorry will be arriving tonight." Petrela held out a piece of paper. Gray got nearer, took it. "All the details are on there."

Gray put the scrap in his pocket. "Thanks."

"Prifti will be in the snooker club at that time. He always is when a delivery is on."

"What about Krisniqi?" It was him Gray really wanted.

"It depends. Sometimes yes, others no."

"Do you want to see your cousin?"

"It's too risky."

"We'll have Krisniqi under arrest soon."

Petrela shook her head. "It's not just Krisniqi. There's one of your men too."

"The informer?"

"Yes."

"What's his name?"

"I don't know, but he came into the snooker club several times and played a couple of games. I saw him talking with Krisniqi once, out the back. He had a tattoo on his arm. Of a shield and two horses, sort of." Petrela showed him her phone. "Like this." Gray recognised it immediately. The crest for Newcastle United football club.

"Would you be willing to testify about what you've seen?"

Petrela laughed but without humour. "Never. As soon as this is over my cousin and me will be leaving the UK and not coming back. I wish you luck." She turned and walked away.

"E," called Gray, but Petrela ignored him and was swallowed up in the gloom.

Back out on the street and in some decent light Gray read the location. He didn't know where it was so checked the map app on his phone. A truck stop.

It made sense as a rendezvous point because the lorry could simply pull off the dual carriageway. The tachometer would show a pause in driving, a legal requirement these days, but no detour.

The location was at least forty-five minutes' drive away out in the countryside towards London. Gray got moving back to the station, placing a call while he was walking.

"You should be the last person I'm hearing from," said Lowther when he answered. "After getting my operative killed.

You wiped out months of effort. All because you didn't speak to me first."

"The plan wasn't for Myerscough to die and he was working for you reluctantly, at best."

"I'm sure." Lowther coughed. "So, are you ringing to apologise? Because I'm not interested. Your DCI did all of that for you."

"Actually, I've got an offer."

"I can't think of anything you could have that'd be of sufficient value to me."

"Hear me out," said Gray.

"You've thirty seconds."

Gray got more than his half minute.

WHEN HE REACHED THE station Gray went straight up to see Hamson. She was on the phone. She covered the handset and mouthed, "What?"

Gray crossed to her desk, pressed a finger down on the phone's contacts, cutting the connection.

"What the hell are you doing, Sol? I was on a conference call with Marsh!"

"I need an urgent word."

"And it couldn't wait?"

"That's what urgent means."

Hamson sat back, steepled her fingers. "This had better be good."

"How about the opportunity to clear up the Albanian gang and the informer at the same time?"

"Okay, that qualifies."

"I had a call from Lowther," lied Gray. "He's received some intelligence that another drugs consignment is coming in tonight. There's going to be a handover. At a truck stop just off the A2, approximately halfway between Dover and Canterbury."

Hamson raised her hand. "We're not doing that all over again."

"It's okay, Lowther is going to handle it. We're not going anywhere near."

"Good."

"What I want is a warrant to raid the snooker club. I have it on good authority that Prifti will be there, maybe Krisniqi too. When Lowther goes in, so do we. I'll grab Prifti and as many of his people as possible."

"What about the informer?"

"He falls into place after the raid. Get Krisniqi, stem the leak."

"Do it," said Hamson.

Forty Two

There was nobody outside the snooker hall when Gray walked up to the door. He headed up the stairs, Airwave radio in one hand, warrant in his pocket. He emerged into the large open area in almost identical circumstances to the last time.

Men leaned over tables, others stood holding a cue, beer or cigarette depending on the state of play. The soft snick of balls striking balls sounded. Gray threaded between the tables, heading for the bar area. The players paused, observing Gray's progress.

Prifti, the gang's leader, was behind the bar once more, polishing a glass. But Gray couldn't see Krisniqi. Prifti smiled as Gray approached. "Detective Inspector Solomon Gray, a pleasure as always. Would you like to sign up to join our club?" Prifti's English was very good, an accent, but not much of one.

"Where's Krisniqi?" asked Gray.

"Maybe just a beer then? On the house of course." Prifti moved to a pump, ready to dispense a drink.

"Krisniqi."

"I don't know who you're talking about."

Gray heard shuffling behind him. A glance over his shoulder showed him the players had moved nearer and were listening, just like before. Gray's finger hovered over the send button of his radio, but for now he held back.

"Your second in command and the man you were speaking to when I was here a few days ago. Surely your memory isn't that bad?"

"I'm just a bartender, Solomon." Prifti clicked his fingers. "I forget, my apologies. You prefer Sol, right?"

"I have records from your homeland which show very clearly what you are."

"A case of mistaken identity. It happens."

Gray put a hand inside his pocket, watched closely all the time by Prifti. Gray laid the paper on the bar. "This is a warrant to search the premises."

"All by yourself? It'll take a while. Then again, I'd heard you were the type who takes on too much personally."

A phone rang behind the bar. Gray said, "You may want to get that."

"If you don't mind?" asked Prifti. He picked up a mobile, flicked a finger across the screen then put it to his ear. He listened for a few seconds before slowly reversing the process.

"Bad news?" Lowther should have carried out the raid on Prifti's truck by now. Gray thumbed the radio button.

"I'll survive."

"Like rats or cockroaches, do you mean?"

Suddenly energised, Prifti dropped the glass and turned to run. But Gray was already on the move. Prifti made for a rear fire exit just as the door to the snooker hall burst open, smacking back into the wall. Prifti's attention was drawn to the noise but Gray knew exactly what it was.

"Police! Stay where you are!"

Prifti shouldered his way through the exit, Gray just a few feet behind. He caught the door on the inswing and was through as Prifti reached the top step of a set of metal stairs on a gloomy hallway. Gray threw himself at Prifti, managing to clip the man's ankle in a trip tackle. Prifti stumbled and went down a couple of steps. Gray got to his feet and propelled himself forward again, hitting Prifti in the small of his back as he rose.

The two men tumbled down the short flight onto a landing. Prifti hit the floor hard beneath Gray, air whooshed out of his lungs. Gray grabbed Prifti's hair and banged his face hard into the metal. Prifti yelped in pain. Gray rolled him over, got hold of his shirt in a bunched fist before headbutting him. Prifti's nose burst under Gray's forehead and the Albanian leader fell back, holding his face between both hands.

Gray pulled the unresisting Prifti to his feet, cuffed his hands behind his back. Blood was coursing from his broken nose, soaking the front of his shirt. Gray manoeuvred Prifti to the top step, his feet over the edge, keeping a grip on the Albanian. Beneath them the steps dropped away steeply. It was a long way to the bottom and Prifti wouldn't have the use of his arms to save himself.

"I could throw you down the stairs and nobody would care," said Gray. He shuffled Prifti forwards half a step.

"No, you wouldn't."

"You're clearly not that well informed about me." Prifti glanced downwards, then grinned at Gray. "You murdered twelve people."

"I didn't touch anybody."

Gray jerked a resisting Prifti forward a little more. It was only Gray's grip stopping Prifti from falling now. "Who have you been working with at my station?" he asked.

"You may as well throw me down, inspector. If I say anything I'm as good as dead anyway."

"It was Worthington, right?"

Prifti grinned. "Come on, Sol. Do it."

Gray almost let go. Almost allowed Prifti to plunge down to certain serious injury and maybe even death. It was the least he deserved. The fire door opened and a uniform poked his head through the gap. "Are you all right, sir?"

"I'm fine."

"We've got everybody rounded up and we're searching the place now."

"Okay."

The uniform retreated back into the hall. The door banged shut.

Gray pulled Prifti back from the edge.

"Such a disappointment, inspector."

"Arian Prifti, I'm arresting you under suspicion of murder."

GRAY WAS IN THE PASSENGER seat of a squad car, following the van transporting Prifti to the station when his phone rang.

Lowther. "Did you get him?" he asked.

"Yes," said Gray.

"Congratulations. Don't expect him to talk, though."

"I've already learned as much. How about you?"

"Relatively successful. However, Krisniqi evaded us."

"Jesus."

"We've got an APB out but thought I'd let you know."

"Thanks."

"Take this totally the way it sounds, inspector, I sincerely hope we never speak again."

"I couldn't agree more." Gray disconnected. He scrolled through his contacts until he reached the one he wanted and dialled. "Hello, Roza, we're bringing him."

ROZA WAS WAITING AT the rear of the building when the convoy drew to a halt. She was leaning against the wall, shoulder hunched, arms crossed. Like she'd fall down if she didn't have support. Gray joined her as the rear door of the truck was opened and Prifti stepped down.

Prifti grinned as he was led past Roza. She took a step forward and spat straight in his face. Prifti didn't bother to wipe the spittle away, just carried on smiling as he was taken inside.

"That felt good," she said. "Thank you for capturing him."

"There's a long way to go yet. Look, I haven't been entirely honest with you."

"Solomon, whatever it is you've got to say to me, I don't care. All that matters is Prifti being jailed." She held her hand out. Gray took it and shook.

Forty Three

Gray found Worthington stepping out of a toilet stall. Before the DC could speak Gray grabbed him by the collar, a bunch of his clothes in Gray's fist. He shoved Worthington hard up against the wall.

Worthington had his arms raised, as if in surrender. "What the f...?" he spluttered.

Gray punched Worthington in the solar plexus, doubling the DC over. He sagged onto his knees, fighting for breath. Gray pushed him in the shoulder and he fell sideways onto the floor, curled up.

"I know it was you," said Gray.

Worthington glanced sideways at him. "What?" he asked between heaves.

"Feeding the Albanians information." Worthington made to rise, but Gray pushed him back down. "At first I thought it was Roza, but it couldn't be. She didn't know enough. It wasn't me, or Hamson or Pfeffer. Then someone said they'd seen you at the club, they described your tattoo."

"Bollocks," said Worthington.

"I'm as certain as I can be that it was you who jumped me in my garage, trying to put me off the investigation as a way of gaining favour with your paymasters. The typed note rather than speaking because I'd have recognised your voice. I'm going to have you hauled up for this."

Worthington got up onto his knees, glared at Gray. "Good luck with that," he said. "Where's the evidence?"

"You're right, I can't prove anything. The thing is, I've only got to be lucky once. Whereas you..." Gray swung back a leg then kicked Worthington in the balls. The DC squealed and curled into a foetal position, teeth bared in pain. Gray squatted down. "I'm making you a promise, Constable Worthington. From now on I'll be right on your shoulder, watching everything. Don't bother applying for a transfer because I'll block it." Gray bent over, spoke into Worthington's ear. "You're mine, until I catch you red handed, *you're mine*."

As Gray was leaving the bathroom a young PC entered. He stopped dead, did a double take, glancing between Gray and Worthington.

"He got his dick caught in his zip," said Gray.

Forty Four

A couple of hours later Gray was at the hospital, sitting in a chair beside Pfeffer. She lay on her back, unconscious still. The monitor was gone, however the drip remained. The mask was gone from her face and the bruises were starting to yellow already. She seemed peaceful.

The door opened, Dr Herbertson entered. "Inspector Gray," he said. "Excuse me, I'm just here to check up on Miss Pfeffer."

"Go ahead." Gray stood. "How is she?"

Herbertson picked up Pfeffer's chart. "Through the worst and improving, I'd say."

"That's great news."

"Miss Pfeffer was awake for a few minutes earlier which is very positive." Herbertson returned the chart then began checking Pfeffer's vital signs. "We carried out another brain scan and there's going to be no lasting damage." Herbertson finished his tests. "Well, all seems to be fine. Now, if you'll excuse me." The doctor left.

Gray sat back down again. He leant back, stared at the ceiling. "Thank God."

"Sol?"

Gray turned. Pfeffer was looking at him. He leant over, took her hand in his, said, "You look well."

She smiled weakly. "And you're talking crap. I feel bloody awful. I've had some fantastic dreams, though."

"That'll be the morphine."

She licked her lips. "Could you pass me some water, please?"

A plastic jug of tepid water stood on the bedside cabinet. Gray poured a glass. She hitched herself up a little, helped by Gray before he handed over the glass and she took a couple of sips. "Thanks." She handed the glass back. "You'll want to know what happened, of course."

"Only if you feel like it."

"I'll live."

"Who did this to you, was it Myerscough?"

She shook her head. "Not long after you left the car doors were pulled open. They weren't locked because the engine was off. Myerscough and me were yanked out. There were four of them, three were wearing masks, but Krisniqi wasn't. He was furious, shouting at Myerscough, wanting to know who'd come for him. Mysercough tried to escape but he had no chance and they bundled him into a van. I tried to stop them, somebody hit me in the face and I went down. I was kicked in the stomach a few times and I blacked out. The next thing I know I'm in here." Pfeffer passed a hand over her face. "I'm sorry. It was all so fast."

"There was nothing more you could do."

"Where is Myerscough?"

"We found him the next day. He'd been tortured before having his throat cut."

"Oh my God." What little colour there had been in Pfeffer's face faded. "Why was he killed?"

"We're guessing retribution, but don't know for sure yet. We got Prifti earlier."

"I'm glad to hear it. What about Krisniqi?"

"He's on the run. Don't worry, we'll get him soon."

"I know." Pfeffer's eyelids began to droop.

Gray stood. "I'll leave you alone, Melanie." He wasn't sure if he should kiss her, and if he did, then where? On the lips, the forehead? In the end he put a hand on her forearm and said, "I'll come back and see you soon." She nodded and closed her eyes.

Outside, Gray leant against the wall, his legs weak. Pfeffer was going to be okay.

Forty Five

It was another two days before Gray got the call.

A body found floating a few miles off the coast, face down, arms splayed. Frayed ropes around the ankles, as if the corpse had been weighed down before coming loose. A photo had arrived at the station and Gray had recognised the man straight away.

"Bad storm last night," said Clough, the pathologist. Behind him stood an ambulance and two paramedics, waiting.

The wind blew hard across the Ramsgate harbour, making the moored yachts bob on choppy waves.

"So I heard," said Gray.

The lifeboat, orange livery bright even in the twilight gloom, made its way slowly towards them. When a few feet from the harbour wall the boat's engine revved hard in reverse, slowing the momentum until the prow barely kissed the quay. Ropes were thrown to waiting men and the lifeboat tied up.

Soon, the body bag was brought up onto deck, unloaded from the ship and placed onto a gurney from the ambulance.

"I want to be sure," said Gray as the gurney neared.

"Of course," replied Clough. He stopped the paramedics, unzipped the bag, revealing just the pale, wrinkled face. "Obviously at this stage we won't know cause of death." The eye sockets were empty, face open in an apparent scream.

Gray didn't care how Krisniqi had expired, just that he was dead and the process had been painful. Retribution for failure from Krisniqi's mafia leaders. A fitting end.

"Sol?" asked Clough.

"That's him," said Gray.

Clough zipped the body bag closed. Gray followed the ambulance to the hospital and went to tell Pfeffer the good news.

THE END

If you want to sign up to a periodic newsletter with information on launches, special offers etc. (no spam!) then you can do so HERE[1].

In return is a *free* book in the Konstantin series, **Russian Roulette**, a unique and gritty crime thriller featuring an ex-KGB operative living undercover in Margate. This is the blurb:

Konstantin Boryakov has just landed in England, a fugitive from the Russian authorities. He ends up in a run-down seaside town where trouble is always just round the corner.

Trouble has a habit of seeking out Konstantin Boryakov, whether he wants it or not. Starting from the moment he arrives in the seedy seaside town of Margate where he's supposed to be in hiding from his Russian ex-employers. Konstantin has to overcome the drug dealer, the loan shark and Fat Gary, all round idiot. Then there's the so-called good guys, the councillors and lawyers who are worse than the criminals.

All Konstantin wants is to be left alone. But it's not to be. Enter Fidelity Brown, aka Plastic Fantastic, the dildo wielding dominatrix who has her own mélange of secrets and lies, and nightclub owner Ken who's connected to all the wrong people.

---

1. https://mailchi.mp/4bbaf7efe867/keith-nixon-free-book

Both help the Russian with the heap of problems delivered to his doorstep.

Cue deception, murder, mayhem as Konstantin settles into his new life. Margate will never be the same again. And neither will Konstantin...

Meet Konstantin Boryakov, the enigmatic ex-KGB agent and tramp with a dark history and darker future in the start of a unique crime thriller series. Pick up *Russian Roulette* to find out what all the fuss is about.

Other Novels By Keith Nixon

The Solomon Gray Series
Dig Two Graves
Burn The Evidence
Beg For Mercy
Bury The Bodies
Pity The Dead

The Konstantin Series
Russian Roulette
The Fix
I'm Dead Again
Dark Heart, Heavy Soul

The Harry Vaughan Series
The Nudge Man

The DI Granger Series
The Corpse Role

The Caradoc Series
The Eagle's Shadow
The Eagle's Blood

About The Author

Keith Nixon is a British born writer of crime and historical fiction novels. Originally, he trained as a chemist, but Keith is now in a senior sales role for a high-tech business. Keith currently lives with his family in the North West of England.

Readers can connect with Keith on various social media platforms:

Web: http://www.keithnixon.co.uk
Twitter: @knntom[1]
Facebook: Keithnixonauthor[2]
Blog: www.keithnixon.co.uk/blog[3]

---

1. https://twitter.com/knntom
2. https://www.facebook.com/keithnixonauthor/
3. http://www.keithnixon.co.uk/blog

Pity The Dead
Published by Gladius Press 2018
Copyright © Keith Nixon 2019
First Edition

Keith Nixon has asserted his right under the Copyright, Designs and Patents Act 1998 to be identified as the author of this work

CONDITIONS OF SALE

All rights reserved. No part of this publication may be reproduced, stored in a retrieval system, or transmitted in any form or by any means, electronic, mechanical, photocopying, scanning, recording or otherwise, without the prior permission of the publisher

This book has been sold subject to the condition that it shall not, by way of trade or otherwise, be lent, resold, hired out, or otherwise circulated without the publisher's prior consent in any form of binding or cover other than that in which it is published and without a similar condition including this condition being imposed on the subsequent purchaser.

All characters in this publication are fictitious and any resemblance to real persons, living or dead is purely coincidental.

Cover design by Jim Divine.

Page of 149

6th April 2019 D6

Don't miss out!

Visit the website below and you can sign up to receive emails whenever Keith Nixon publishes a new book. There's no charge and no obligation.

https://books2read.com/r/B-A-BGNH-ZUUY

BOOKS 2 READ

Connecting independent readers to independent writers.

Did you love *Pity The Dead*? Then you should read *The Nudge Man* by Keith Nixon!

A washed up reporter, an escaped convict, a sociopathic gangster. All are hunting The Nudge Man...

Wheelchair bound, born again, ex-gangster, Eric Hennessey offers down on his luck reporter, Harrison Vaughan, a job. Find The Nudge Man, a mysterious vigilante who's stolen most of Hennessey's money, ill-gotten gains which now Hennessey wants to use to do God's work. Trouble is, Harry has no desire to work for a sociopathic murderer, even if he is apparently changed man.

Harry is estranged from his family, he hasn't seen or heard from them in over five years, since a fabricated scandal destroyed his career. Harry believes his wife walked out on him and took the children. However, Hennessey tells Vaughan it was The Nudge Man who set him up for the fall. Find The Nudge Man and Harry has the chance for redemption and maybe even his family back.

However, Hennessey has another objective in mind. Unknown to Harry his family were taken into witness protection and had to cut ties with everyone after Harry's son saw a murder – carried out by Eric Hennessey. But the witness protection programme was compromised and the Vaughans had to go off the grid, they couldn't contact anybody. Hennessey has been looking for them ever since and now may have a way in – Harry himself.

Harry's search begins in prison, visiting violent criminal Pomfrey Lavender – apparently Lavender has information which will help. But Lavender is suffering various medical problems, including a psychological condition whereby he believes he's already dead. Harry's mention of The Nudge Man sends Lavender into a rage and he threatens to kill Harry should he pursue his objective. Harry is relieved Lavender is behind bars. Trouble is, two days later Lavender breaks out.

And others are on the trail of The Nudge Man, including the British government and an American secret service agent. Then there's the lawyer who offers Harry £1m. All Harry has to do is stay away from The Nudge Man.

With more questions than answers and hapless guard dog, Bonzo at his side who's bark is definitely worse than his bite, Harry begins his search.

Can Harry find The Nudge Man and save his family? Or will Hennessey exact his revenge?

"Packed with the author's trademark wit, The Nudge Man is a seriously good, mind-bendingly twisty novel, and cements Nixon's place among the upper echelon of British crime writers."*M.W. Craven, author of the Washington Poe Novels.*

What Readers Say

What Readers Say'A great story that unfolded at a perfect pace."The twists and turns keep one gripped and the ending, totally unexpected, will knock your socks off."A black comedy crime thriller with a difference."If you want to give someone the gift that keeps on giving, buy them a copy of The Nudge Man."A fantastic read with some great characters."Highly recommended 5 stars.'

Also by Keith Nixon

Caradoc
The Eagle's Shadow
The Eagle's Blood

Detective Solomon Gray
Dig Two Graves
Burn The Evidence
Beg For Mercy
Bury The Bodies
Pity The Dead

DI Granger
The Corpse Role

Gray Box Set

The Solomon Gray Series: Books 1 - 4: Gripping Police Thrillers With A Difference

Harrison Vaughan
The Nudge Man

Konstantin
Russian Roulette
The Fix
I'm Dead Again
Dark Heart, Heavy Soul

Standalone
The Solomon Gray Series: Books 1 to 4: Gripping Police Thrillers With A Difference

Printed in Great Britain
by Amazon